MW01169570

# Tell No Lie,

# We Watched

# Her Die

## Richard Sanders

>>>

>>>

The Mongol suit of armor featured mirrors over the heart, in the belief that mirrors could deflect and even destroy evil forces, such as enemy spears, simply by reflecting them.

—Laurence Bergreen, *Marco Polo: From Venice to Xanadu*

# >>>CHAPTER 1

## >>DARKNESS
## ALL AROUND

**THE LAST TIME**
**SHE'LL BE SEEN ALIVE**

It started like any other piece of home-shot video. Blurry, patchy, grainy, underlit. TV on in the background, its transmission lines rippling with static. Bright blotches of jewelry scattered on the counter next to the TV. For the first few seconds the television audio is the clearest thing about the image: It's the 6 p.m. newscast from KTTV, the Fox affiliate in Los Angeles.

Then the fleshy smudges in the foreground take on definition and shape. The lens is adjusting to the low light. There's movement, moaning. You see a man's body lying on a bed. A woman, a brunette, is going down on him, her bobbing head positioned in the center of the frame. Okay, so what's the deal? It's just somebody's amateur porn.

Why was this forwarded to me?

But 12, 13 seconds into it, the woman raises her head. She looks up at her partner and smiles at him, checking his reaction. That's when you realize this isn't simply some random tape. There are the pouty, heart-curved lips, famously kept plump with Blistex balm. There's the brown mole just above the left side of her upper lip. There are the eyes—large, almond-shaped and somehow, despite her life, peaceful. There's the mermaid tattoo on her right shoulder, the tattoo they tried to hide with body makeup for her nude scenes in *I'm Still Waiting* but finally had to digitally conceal.

No mistake: It's Amanda Eston. It's the Disney darling who turned tween and teen queendom into a film career filled with sweaty-palmed reviews and movies that routinely grossed $100 million plus. It's the actress who managed to hold onto her sweetheart fanbase despite emotional breakdowns, mood swings, episodes of depression, drunken displays, drug overdoses, emergency hospital visits and prolonged rehab stays.

The man's face is never seen. All you can catch are snatches of his chest, hips, thighs. His one claim to video fame: A large, wine-colored, football-shaped birthmark on the side of his average-size cock. Otherwise he's anonymous. The fixed camera is angled to showcase Amanda Eston's performance. The focus stays on her, in porn as in life.

She goes back to work, providing more lip service. All right—this is mildly, if grimly, interesting. It's high-wattage erotica and you watch it with a kind of breathless voyeurism, though what you're seeing is oddly tranquil for sex.

Then there's a moment when it all turns.

It comes from the sound on the TV. In the course of reporting a story, one of the newscasters mentions the day's date and year. And if you know anything about Amanda Eston, you know that her body will be found hours later. In this same room. In this same bed.

If you know anything about Amanda Eston, you know this is the last time she'll be seen alive.

She was discovered in her bedroom five years ago at 11:47 p.m., on the same day this tape was made. Large amounts of a rare drug called pralicin were found in her system. According to the ME, she died of acute pralicin poisoning. Her death was ruled to be an accidental overdose, though listed as a possible suicide.

But in the lab of public opinion the story didn't end there. The weeks that followed her death brought darker talk, tales of suspicious behavior, strange silences, gaps and inconsistencies in the police reports, disputed autopsy findings, secret phone calls, missing records, mysterious visitors. More than one media outlet ran features asking *Who Killed Amanda Eston?*

Much of the suspicion centered on a flamboyant and conspicuously married politician named Robby Walsh, then governor of Nevada. Walsh and Amanda were loudly rumored to be having an affair, at the same time he was under investigation for fraud and conspiracy. Six months after her death, Robby Walsh was convicted on RICO racketeering charges and served three years as a guest of the federal government. He now worked as a lobbyist.

It was Amanda's ex, the actor L.C. Martin, who led the attack on Walsh. Briefly married to the actress (they barely lasted a year), Martin went all over the media, claiming that Amanda knew something about Walsh's illegal activities, she knew too much, she might've known about even bigger things he was involved in, and that's why he'd had her killed. Her death, Martin openly said, was a murder staged to look like a drug overdose.

And now you're looking at the prelude to her death, the foreshadowing of her end. Everything about the video—the grain, the blurs—has been touched by what's going to happen.

This isn't porn anymore. Porn keeps you out, keeps you watching the performers as objects. But this thing, this pulls you in. This draws you into itself. This makes you feel connected to what you're seeing, as if hidden messages are being carried through the bytes and bandwidth and are entering your body through your eyes.

Which explains why this one minute and 18 second video is on your screen. Which explains why it was posted on a small, obscure site in Amsterdam and picked up worldwide in a record 30 minutes.

It's infused with dreamspun danger, with night and terror. You know what's coming. You know what's going to happen. You know that death is rushing through every frame.

## A PINHOLE SPHINCTER

I found my boss, Louisa Collins, sitting in one of the armchairs in her office, a can of Diet Coke in her hand, staring at the gray Hudson River outside her windows. The big woman was in a pensive mood.

"You okay?"

Slow, slow nod. "I'm just pondering some of the deeper questions. Like why does Coke foam up but Sprite doesn't? Things like that."

"I'm trying to remember what Wittgenstein said about it."

She took a heavy breath and turned away from the view. "You find a contact?"

"His name's Arnoud Shuyler, based in Amsterdam. He says the full video's 11 minutes. Lotta material."

"He's the owner?"

"No, a go-between. He's conducting the auction."

"We know anything about him?"

"Not a whole lot. He seems to traffic in some of the more *outlying* markets. There was a couple of pieces of stolen art recovered—he was the middleman. He also apparently deals in twisty film clips, pieces of video. Stuff that doesn't get widely seen."

"Blackmail?"

"It's never been proved."

Louisa looked like a migraine had suddenly infected her skull. "I don't want to get in bed with this guy, but I don't see another choice. We need the video. We have to have it."

She spoke with a constricted throat and zero enthusiasm, and I understood why. The *Real Story* franchise—the magazine and website—was doing well, but ad sales were still hurting and the lack affected almost every decision. We used to work in an intense but loose atmosphere. Then it became more tight-ass. Now it was like a pinhole sphincter.

"Eleven minutes," said Louisa. "We could chop it up, fuzz out the naughty bits, package it in dozens of ways. We could make a lot of money with it."

"It's in-person bidding only, at least for the opening round. Show of commitment. I can get the London bureau chief there in a couple hours."

"No." On a note of finality. "No, I want you to do it."

She outlined her reasons. As usual, they were sound. I'd worked as a licensed investigator in a previous career incarnation—that might make me better qualified to deal with somebody like Arnoud Shuyler. I was also a recovering alcoholic and crystal-meth addict—that might make me qualified to deal with any friends or family of Amanda Eston, should they get involved. Both qualifications, in fact, were intertwined. I'd lost my license by getting so fucked up on booze and meth I'd killed a guy one long-ago night, ended up doing time for manslaughter and took a chance at redemption by writing and eventually editing for *Real Story*.

"What're the parameters?" I said.

"Start at 10 million. Take it up to 20 if you have to. Call me if it goes higher."

And that, as they say, was that. It felt right to me, no question. She was right about my background. My feet knew this path.


>>>

## THE MOMENT

Arnoud Shuyler lived just a few blocks from the Rembrantplein. Would've been a simple cab ride from the hotel, but no. He insisted I drive there myself. He didn't want involvement from any traceable third parties like taxi drivers. That was part of the deal. So I had to rent a car and negotiate strange streets, concentric canals and the two-wheeled jungle of this city of inveterate bicycle riders. Plus pay a parking fee that cost about as much as I'd probably pay for the video.

His building was four stories of solid stone, neo-baroque style, decorated to the high heavens with pre-kitsch ornamentation. You don't see a lot of this in Hell's Kitchen.

Arnoud answered the door himself. He was a balding white-haired man with a body so rotund his arms could never fall below a 45-degree angle. He was wearing a satin gold Nehru jacket. Striking.

Facially, he looked like a big blissful baby who'd just finished his bottle. Hard to tell his real age. He'd had work done around the eyes and chin.

In accented English he told me how happy he was to have a reputable operation like *Real Story* in the mix, and as he led me inside he speculated on the Irish origins of my name, Quinn McShane.

Arnoud took me into the ornate, double-doored drawing room of the house, a space about as large as the master stateroom on Commodore Vanderbilt's yacht. High ceiling, tall windows lined with velour drapes, polished mahogany-paneled walls hung with Flemish and French tapestries, heavy carpeting, Victorian furniture covered in Protestant velvet. Very Dutch plush.

He offered me an afternoon cognac. I passed. He poured himself a snifter and waddled over to a small table with carved wooden cranes suspended between its legs. A laptop, the room's single bow to modernity, sat on the top. He called up the Amanda Eston video he'd posted early yesterday, the sex shot seen 'round the world.

"Clever marketing gimmick," I said.

"Yes, I thought it would be effective, draw attention. There is, as you can imagine, a great deal of demand."

"I can imagine that."

He sipped his brandy and chuckled. "So strange, you know, the value we put on things. Let me ask. How much would you pay for a square foot of asbestos?"

"Not a whole hell of a lot."

"And yet, centuries ago, asbestos was worth its equal in gold. It was considered a precious material, valuable enough to be woven into the burial shrouds of the Eastern kings. Time changes everything."

Arnoud played the video. There it was again, the room, the shadows, the TV in the background, the vertical movement of Amanda's head. This must've been the 18th time I'd seen it.

"What's the provenance?" I said.

"It was recently found by an American collector, found among a vagrant's possessions. The belongings were unclaimed, as I understand, and were being auctioned by a storage warehouse."

"Who's the collector?"

"I can't give you the name, I'm, afraid. Not at liberty."

Despite all the carpeting and drapes and velvet and tapestries in the room, you could still hear an echo trailing our voices.

The show ran its minute and 18 seconds and reached the end.

"No need to mention the great historical value here," said Arnoud, refilling his snifter. "Anyone curious about her life, and her death, will find this of interest."

"Agreed."

"And so we arrive at it, the moment. What do I hear?"

"Ten million."

He was staring at the computer screen. "I would describe the bidding at this stage as extraordinary. It's even *desperate*—I wouldn't feel uncomfortable saying that."

"Twelve million."

"I must tell you, the interest in this goes beyond anything I've ever seen. I would go so far as to call it *paranormal*—I believe that's the word."

"Fifteen million."

Arnoud nodded and turned away from the laptop. "We're off to a good start. Very nice. Yes, very nice."

"You're happy with 15."

"At this point, quite so. At this point the first round comes to a close. I'll keep you up to date of course on the progress of the competing bids. Feel free to return to New York."

"What else is on the tape? For 15 I'd like to get a little better idea."

"I suppose so. Yes, 15 should buy you a little extra peek. I can show you two more minutes."

He clicked another icon. This segment picked up where the other one left off. Amanda, dining time over, climbs up on the bed, straddles the man and begins rocking herself on his cock. His face still can't be seen. It's all her.

"Such a sad fate she had," said Arnoud. He finished off the second snifter. "So much darkness in the world these days, you know? Darkness all around, Mr. McShane. All around. So much darkness these days that some people can't even see it. So much darkness they think they're still looking at the light."

>>>

## GO FUCKING YOURSELF

Sun going down, street lights coming down. I drove past bars, restaurants, café terraces, bicyclists, bike racks, alleyways, neo-gothic buildings that looked like miniature fortresses, doors and windows built in weird shapes.

Stopping at a light, I took out my cell and checked the tape I'd made of Arnoud's conversation. It wasn't a question of trusting him—I didn't. I just wanted a record of what was and wasn't said.

It was all there, including his *darkness these days* soliloquy.

I wasn't so sure about the darkness. People are always thinking that things were better in the past, but how can that be? How about the time when people stopped hunting and started growing food from the ground? They were ending a tradition that had gone on for tens of thousands of years and swapped it for something that no living creature had ever done before. You don't think that was culture shock? You don't think people sat around talking about *darkness these days*? They were saying, oh life was so much better when the men took their spears into the forest and the women stayed home and cooked the meat. People knew their places back then and we didn't have all this confusion.

I think I'm going to ying-yang it: There's always been the same amount of darkness and light in the world, the two forces dancing with each other in equal balance.

I'd stopped at another light when I saw the car again. A sky-blue Audi TT, coming out of the twilight two cars in back of me. This was the third time I'd noticed

it since leaving Arnoud's, always
maintaining a discreet distance behind.

Test it out. I made a turn and drove
through a series of small out-of-the-way
streets. The view: stone walls, people
smoking and staring into space, a bar with
patrons loudly singing inside. A boxspring
and mattress had been left out on the curb
of one street. A homeless guy was
sleeping on it, no one paying any attention
to him.

The Audi TT was still behind me.

I went back to a main road, slowed
for a red light. Three cars pulled into my
lane. I saw the Audi turn a corner and
make an approach toward the last car.

The light was still red. No
oncoming traffic. I shifted into reverse,
swung my wheel around and gunned the
gas, lurching into the oncoming lane. I
shot backward past the three cars, cut my

wheel again and slammed to a stop sideways in the lane, just inches away from the Audi's front grill and blocking its path. Horns went off. Bikers scattered.

I jumped out and went for the Audi. The driver, a fish-faced guy with a black leather skull cap, was sitting in a muddled daze, not moving.

But talking.

"What's the matter with you you fucking crazy!"

His English was much more accented than Arnoud's. But how did he know I spoke English? We all look alike?

"You mind telling me what's going on?" I said. "I'd just like to know."

"You motherfucker! You should drive more careful."

"What do you want?"

"What do I want? I don't want nothing. I'm not bothering you, no problem."

"You're following me, you're bothering me."

"I beg your pardon? Excuse me? I'm not following nobody."

"I don't believe you."

"Go fucking yourself."

"What're you up to?"

By now two other cars had quietly slipped behind the Audi. Then a tire-squealing BMW pulled up fast into the lane and braked to a stop. Its driver, a guy with an overcoat and a gaunt Storm Trooper's face, bolted out of the door. He smiled at me and waved.

"Hallo!" he said. "You like to talk the sports?"

Not in this situation, not particularly, but before I could say anything he reached inside his coat and pulled something out. I could see the gun like he was standing next to me.

Two bullets tore into the Audi's roof. Another popped off my hood.

I ran for it. No way to get back to my car. I hit the sidewalk, the pavement bulging and rippling, as gunshots ricocheted off the walls. The sound of a pair of pounding feet were hard behind me.

A building with a fire-gutted front stood 20 feet away. An alley opened right next to it. I jerked into the turn. In the middle of the alley a kid was spray-painting red graffiti on an open metal door.

The Storm Trooper guy reached the alley nine seconds later. Halfway up, just as he passed the door, I swung it open and yelled *hey*. When he whirled around I sprayed a good gush of red paint in his eyes. Blinded, he went to raise his gun. I kicked him in the stomach and chopped him in the back of the neck. The gun fell to the ground. So did he.

The kid crept out of the doorway. I gave him back the paint and the euros I'd promised, picked up the gun and went back to the street. The Audi was gone.

I jogged to my car and took off, stopping a couple minutes later to toss the gun in one of the canals. Thinking: What the hell was this? Some kind of bizarre random coincidence? Or something connected like conjoined twins to my visit with Arnoud Shuyler?

>>>

## THREE CALLS

By the time I got back to New York, I was
casting a heavy vote for the connection
theory. Louisa showed me the reports from
European sites: Arnoud was dead. He'd
been shot inside his home, discovered a
few hours after I'd left him. The
Amsterdam-Amstelland police said the
incident bore all the marks of an attempted
robbery, although they hadn't yet
determined if anything was missing.

*So much darkness in the world
these days. Darkness all around.*

And so much for the Amanda
Eston video. This was one piss-shot effort.

Three hours after I'd landed,
though, I got a call from a Gisela
Westerveldt. She was an officer with van
de Politie Amsterdam-Amstelland,
investigating Arnoud's death. The
appointment calendar they'd found on his

computer showed he was scheduled to meet with me on the afternoon he was killed. Had the meeting taken place, and if so, why?

I told her the truth—I was bidding on the infamous Amanda Eston video. How about other visitors? Did I see anyone in or near the house before or after I'd left? No, but I told her about the Audi and the BMW. Why didn't I report it?

Sorry about that, but considering Arnoud's background, I thought going to the police might kill the deal, so to speak. Gisela wasn't thrilled, but she lightened up a bit when I gave her full descriptions of the fish-faced guy with the skull cap and the gaunt Storm Trooper gunman.

What about phone calls? she said. According to Arnoud's records, I'd made three calls to him. Correct—the first was my initial contact with him, the second to tell him I'd be flying in to see him, the third from the hotel.

Each time I'd called, said Gisela, Arnoud had made a flurry of calls to three other people. Maybe I could help with that.

*Do you know a Heiko Krueger?*

No."

*Farig al-Esayi?*

"No."

*Grady Alexander?*

I hesitated a second. Arnoud's words: *an American collector.*

"No."

We talked a few more minutes. Did Arnoud seem anxious? Uneasy? Overly defensive? No, no and no.

The minute the call ended I started digging for Grady Alexander. I couldn't find a thing, at least not on a Grady Alexander who wasn't deceased. I asked

one of our reporters, Kumiko Davis, a
search genius, for help. Even she had
trouble—there was no listing for him
anywhere, no phone number, no nothing.
All she could come up with was a single
database-buried reference. Two years ago,
Grady Alexander had purchased a parcel
land in LA.

California, here I come.


>>>

# >>>CHAPTER 2

## >>THIS AMNESIA FOG

**PURPLE BLUES**

*Real Story* had a Smithsonian's worth of bio files on Amanda Eston. I spent my flight time going through them, trying to get a better picture of her life.

•She grows up in small-town Virginia, in a family where stability is as rare as money. Her father leaves her mother when Amanda is 3. She and her 1-year-old sister are cared for by a shuttle-bus of relatives, sometimes including her mother.

•Two years later, her father commits suicide.

•Amanda develops an interest in performing, taking every fee community-center class she can find in acting, singing and dancing.

•When Amanda is 9, her mother is committed to a mental institution. The girl and her sister, Tasha, are raised thereafter by their Aunt Renee, their mother's cousin.

•Amanda lands her first professional job, playing a sick child in a commercial for St. Joseph's Aspirin for children. She also finds vocal work in several cartoon specials.

•A day before Amanda's 12th birthday, her mother kills herself in a halfway house.

•At 14, Amanda wins a full scholarship to the Virginia School of the Performing Arts. She becomes a brilliant but troubled student, repeatedly disciplined for drinking, drug use, body piercing and sexual activity. In her junior year she's hospitalized for a drug overdose and expelled from the school. "She was very bright and very talented," one of her teachers says later, "but she couldn't stay away from the dark side."

•At 17, she goes to LA and, lying about her age, gets a job as a Hooter's waitress. After working four months, she auditions for the lead in a new Disney Channel comedy, *Bunny Hops*. She wins the role of Bunny Beresford, a normal middle-school student growing up in a likeably crazy family. *Bunny Hops* eventually draws 2.5 million viewers each episode, turning into the Disney Channel's highest-rated program. Amanda Eston becomes a household tween name.

•After a thee-year run and a blistering disagreement with Disney, Amanda walks away from *Bunny Hops*. She joins the cast of a new teen drama, *The Fit*, about backstabbing students competing in a high school for fashion and design. Reviews are terrible, but the show becomes a widely watched guilty pleasure. Teen girls en masse begin to dress and act like Amanda. Many use makeup to imitate her mole and her fleshy lips. Requests for plastic mouth surgery among teens rises eight percent. In an interview, Amanda says she uses Blistex lip balm to maintain that pouty look. Blistex sales jump 12 percent.

•Meeting a part-time grip in a local bar, Amanda sets off on her first public romance. The on-off affair lasts half a year, until the grip returns to his wife. Paparazzi footage shows Amanda looking dazed and out of it as she stumbles in and out of clubs.

•She launches her own clothing and jewelry line for teens, Amandawear. At a press conference announcing the launch, Amanda is pale and nearly incoherent and close to passing out. Later that week she checks herself into Cedars-Sinai for what her publicist calls exhaustion and a touch of the flu.

•During the holiday season months later, Amanda volunteers at soup kitchens and clothing give-aways. Her new publicist admits the hospitalization was the result of a nervous breakdown. "She realizes that helping people, giving back to the community, is a way to get back to health." Amandawear grosses $5 million during the holidays alone.

•An Amanda Eston story runs on the cover of *Real Story*, the first of many. She wins an Emmy during the second season of *The Fit*, and at the end of the season makes her first film, *The Fit Movie*. It pulls in $40 million on its opening weekend.

•She quickly follows up with *I'm Still Waiting*, a loose remake of the 1962 Sandra Dee comedy, *If A Man Answers*. The film stays in the No. 1 slot for four weeks. Amanda refuses to sign for another season of *The Fit* and takes on a series of older, more challenging movie roles. Most reviewers go into swan-dive swoons.

"You'd go to see some actresses," writes one, "to watch them read the phone book. You'd go to see Amanda Eston just to watch her *thumb* through the phone book." She appears on the cover of *Elle* and is included in *Vanity Fair*'s Annual Hollywood Issue. Six months later she gets her own *Vanity Fair* cover. By then, she's been on five *Real Story* covers.

•Production of her fourth movie, *Faking The Waves*, is delayed when the director insists she gets drug and alcohol treatment. "I don't want to do what they've done with other young actors," he says, "which is give them money to kill themselves." Her treatment doesn't quite take. Amanda begins dating one of her *Faking The Waves* costars and reportedly tries to kill herself with an overdose when filming ends. Rumors of breakdowns and blackouts surface in high volume. She's seen with a new guy every month. She gets engaged but breaks it off two months later, reportedly after suffering a miscarriage.

•In one well-publicized incident, she delays the production of her sixth film, *Call And Response*, when she fails to show up on the set for two weeks. As an excuse, she cites just about every emotional malady listed in the *DSM*. She buys the cast and crew lavish gifts when she comes back to work and makes a large charitable contribution in the producers' names.

•Her younger sister, Tasha, a marketing student, moves to LA to look out for her. Doesn't work. Amanda is arrested on three DUI's in the space of a month. Urged by her new publicist, she issues an apology to her fans. There's no need. Her fanbase understands and forgives her. They see a fragility and loneliness in her, and an almost naïve sense of wonder about the world. Combine that with her reputation for generosity, they treat her like the second incarnation of the Virgin Mary. Her new perfume, *With Love From Amanda*, sets a fragrance-market retail record in the first three months.

•She wins a Golden Globe for *Call And Response*. A day later, she's rushed to the hospital for what her publicist says is a bad reaction to medication. Months later, in an interview arranged by her new publicist, Amanda admits it was an overdose. "I really thought that was it, I was on the way out," she says, "My problem is connecting, connecting with another human being. I just can't do it. I just can't seem to connect with another person."

•She's cast in *Days Of Reckoning*, playing a woman who, trying to reconcile with her father, imagines what he was like in the various stages of his life. Her father is played by an actor her own age, L.C. Martin. They become involved on the first day of filming. "I wasn't even thinking about it," L.C. says, "and I don't think she was either. Our bodies were doing the talking."

•The couple gets married on the set, on the day the film wraps. *Real Story* gets the exclusive. "It's really important to have someone who can remind you who you are," she told us. "I can run myself insane, but he always brings me back. He always lets me know who I really am."

•Her Aunt Renee, who raised her and her sister, dies in Virginia. When Amanda finds out the family doesn't have enough money to bury her, she flies the body and her relatives to LA for the funeral. Renee is interred in a pink marble crypt in a cemetery near Amanda's home.

•After 11 months of marriage, Amanda and L.C. file for divorce. The usual suspect, irreconcilable differences, is cited as the cause.

•At a charity event for the homeless, Amanda passes out. She's admitted to a rehab. "She's come to understand," says her new publicist, "that her ongoing recovery from addiction requires special treatment."

•After three days in rehab, Amanda checks out and disappears. She issues a statement saying that she needs "an extended vacation" and that she's canceling plans for her next movie, *Purple Blues*. Her sister goes on TV and through tears and sobs pleads with Amanda to get help for her "serious emotional problems."

•Back in LA, Amanda reportedly starts seeing Nevada governor Robby Walsh, a politician best known for his fund-raising ability. The rumors are denied on both sides, though Amanda teasingly tells a reporter she's "passionately interested in politics."

•She holds a press conference to announce that *Purple Blues* is back on track. She appears happy and relaxed in what will turn out to be her last public appearance.

•Three nights later, her bodyguard makes a routine call to her house to see if she's all right. There's no answer. Rushing to the house, the bodyguard finds her nude on the bed, face down, with no pulse. The police are called. An overdose of pralicin is ruled as the COD, although no bottles of pralicin or bags containing traces of the drug are found in the house. Police speculate that the drug was bought on the street and immediately ingested.

And then she was buried. I remember her funeral, remember covering the story, remember the hysteria it brought out. One of our more scabrous competitors offered the paps $1 million for a shot of her in her casket. The funeral, as a result, was guarded like a military base. Only 35 guests were invited and they were all subject to searches. Cell phones and pocketbooks had to be surrendered. Undercover security kept watch for the appearance of cameras and recording devices.

Still, it was said to be a beautiful ceremony. The arrangements had been made by L.C. Martin, who said he'd kept in touch with Amanda even after their divorce. L.C. delivered the eulogy, after which a dozen doves were released in the air. Amanda Eston was also interred in a pink marble crypt, on the plot next to her Aunt Renee. Back home again.

>>>

## SPARK THE QUARKS

I checked into the Chateau Marmont, then drove out to the *Real Story* bureau in Brentwood, on Wilshire, and picked up the Fedex package I'd sent to myself. Inside was my Glock 9. I wasn't going to try to find the possible collector without it. After that little dust-up in Amsterdam, after the deal Arnoud Shuyler made with mortality, I felt a need for preventative measures.

Grady Alexander had bought a parcel of land in Topanga Canyon, in the mountains near Malibu. The sun started splitting into endless shafts of light and shadow as I drove up the all-tree terrain. It took about 40 minutes to find the road listed on the title—a reclusive dirt path with as many twists and turns as an elephant's colonoscopy.

Finally I came to a simple, low-walled structure built with plain pine panels, sliding doors and screens, and a thatched roof, surrounded by trees and vines and underbrush years past clearing.

It was like coming across a Shinto temple in the woods.

My knock was answered by a young, long-haired ascetic with a moustache and goatee, wearing a Yukata-style kimono. He walked with a lopsided gait—one of his legs was shorter than the other.

He looked at me like I was loaded down with Jehovah's Witness pamphlets.

"My name's Quinn McShane. From *Real Story*."

Didn't do much for his mood. If his suspicion could kill plantlife, his property would look like the moon.

"I was dealing with Arnoud Shuyler," I went on. "I was dealing with him, sorry to say, just before he died."

"I know. I know who you are." He put his hands inside his kimono pockets. "How did you find me? Nobody's supposed to know who I am."

"It's a gift."

As Grady thought about this, I noticed something about him. Maybe he wasn't exactly stoned, but he was definitely stony.

"My thought was, maybe I can deal directly with you," I said. "Now that the middleman's been eliminated."

No response.

"Of course, I don't know if the video's still around. I don't know if it was stolen from Arnoud's house."

"Arnie never had the original. All he had were clips. I still have it." Quick add: "But not here."

"He told you what we were offering?"

Grady nodded. "Twelve."

Oops. Neither confirm nor deny.

"It's a lot of money," I said. "I'm sure you don't want to pass that up."

"I don't want to do *anything*. Not now. Not after what happened to Arnie. I don't need that level of weirdness."

A ringtone went off. He reached in the kimono for his cell. The music was a sinuous, desert-stark, guitar-trance sound, Middle-Eastern blues. I recognized it: the Libyan group, Tinariwen.

Grady gimped away from the door, taking the call inside. I followed him.

Except for a 54-inch screen on one wall showing lava-lamp images, the furniture was Japanese basic. Small blocky tables. Short wooden benches. The window screens and the trees outside threw shifts of light and shade on the floor.

"I've got some RD-17 coming in," Grady was saying. "It's robust, full-bodied... Yeah, from Perkasa, from the Indonesian guy... It's a little heavier than that, lots of undertones."

Still looking around, I saw a counter loaded with Ziploc bags. Each baggie was labeled and filled with pills. There had to be thousands of capsules sitting there.

"I still have plenty of TT-44... It's very nice, very clean and cool. More topping to it, more *essence*... No, no, just the opposite. Really sparks the quarks in your head. Good for creativity. You want to work on that screenplay, I'd go with the TT... Okay, let me know. I can do you either way."

He dropped the phone back in his robe.

"You deal."

Grady nodded, no hesitation.

"You're pretty open about it."

"Legal product only. No street stuff. I target a more selective market, more I guess you could say *exotic*. Designer drugs, hard to find. I'm in touch with the best chemists and garage labs in the country. It's a whole cottage industry."

"Must be like the early 60s."

"Exactly. That's exactly the vibe. Everything is legal—or not illegal yet. Soon as there's legislation on something, I phase it out of the inventory."

I looked again at the baggie counter. "Make good money?"

"I can flip in the six-figures."

"So you can afford to collect Amanda Eston memorabilia. Amanda Estonia, I think they call it?"

"I frankly don't give a fuck about Amanda Eston."

"Arnoud told me you were a collector."

"I am, but not that. I don't follow pop culture much. It's *inorganic*."

"So what do you collect?"

"It's called bumilia. Though I think that's a derogatory term."

"Bumilia?"

"Stuff owned by homeless people. Here."

He limped to another room and switched on the lights. The walls were lined with glass-enclosed, climate-controlled display cases. Individual spotlights picked out ragged pants, torn sweaters, filthy overcoats, blankets, can openers, eating utensils, cream bath lotions, Handi-Wipes, deodorant, combs, brushes, screwdrivers, switchblades, cigarette lighters, pipes, keys, books, broken dolls, bedraggled stuffed animals,

yellowed letters, driver's licenses,
Medicaid cards, mass cards, crosses on
neck chains, costume jewelry, dog collars,
hand-painted postcards, sculpture made of
beer-can tabs.

"I try to find things that speak to a
life," said Grady. "Sometimes I buy it
direct off the street, sometimes at auction."

"That's where you found the video,
right?"

"A few years ago—three years, it
was—I bid on a pile of stuff from a
storage warehouse. It appeared to belong
to a guy named Norridge Morris, all left
there, unclaimed. This is him."

Grady guided me down to the end
of one of the display cases. Inside were
capes, hoodies and T-shirts painted with
weird, flat, totemic faces. Real outsider-art
stuff. The faces looked like aliens who'd

crash-landed their UFO and were now begging for coin on Fifth Street.

Other items were grouped with the clothes: balls of twine and rubber bands, a small wad of foreign bills, a flask.

"He had a lot of things," said Grady, "not all of it too interesting. One thing I found was a disk of some kind. Still in a jewel box, no label, nothing. Who cares? I forget about it. Couple of months ago I came across it again. Slipped it into the computer, let's see what this is."

"And you saw it.'

"I saw it. I don't know much about entertainment, but I knew who she was. I remember when she died, I remembered the date. Realized, from the TV broadcast, this was the same day. And I realized, holy shit, this is *worth*."

"It's some collectible. You didn't think about keeping it?"

"Means nothing to me. These things"—he gestured to the cases—"these things I would never sell. But this? Why not?'

"So you found Arnoud."

"The world of collectors tends to be pretty connected. I asked around, heard about this guy Arnie Shuyler. Heard he was experienced in selling photos of famous people in what should we call it compromising situations."

The ringtone again. Grady drifted into the rest of the house as he answered.

"Yeah. Yeah, I can do that. How much you looking for?... Not a problem. Seven-fifty for you... Six-seventy-five? I can't do 675. Seven-twenty-five... Can't do it. Six-ninety's no good. My CPM's are too high."

I noticed an inside balcony built into an upper corner at the back of the

house, ladder leading down to the floor.
The top of the balcony poked into and
through the thatched roof like a perfect
bird's nest. Must be his bedroom.
Probably feels like you're sleeping in the
trees up there.

Grady pulled a calculator out of his
pockets and began punching in numbers.
"Seven-fifteen, but you're killing me…
Seven? No way, man. I'm supposed to
*lose* money? Seven-ten, that's the best I
can do. You've got me right on the edge…
Okay? Seven-ten? Okay, we're there…
Right, I'll see you later… Yeah, well, it
takes one to grow one."

The phone and calculator
disappeared in his kimono. He looked at
me.

"So?" I said

"So?"

"Sell me the video. There's no cost-per-thousand involved. It's pure profit."

"I can't."

"Why not?"

He took a seat on one of the small benches and rubbed his eyes for quite a few seconds. "You know what I believe?"

"What's that?"

"I believe we're all linked in this *rhythm*, this vast, all-encompassing rhythm. I believe this rhythm is what keeps the world together. And anything we do—or anything we *don't* do, for that matter—anything we do to affect this rhythm, we'll feel the echo of it further on down the line."

"Okay."

"Okay, so you see the business I run here? There's no guns. There's no hired muscle. There's no dope-dealing violence. I'd like to keep it like that. I don't want any attachment to violence further on down the road."

"What makes you think there would be?"

"What happened to Arnie? Somebody shot him. Somebody gunned him down. He got himself *killed*."

"That might not have anything to do with the video."

"Well he never got himself killed *before*. You see? You see what I'm saying? There's something about this video, there's something *sinister* about it, and I don't want to step into it. So *that's* what I'm saying. I'm not selling anything to anybody, not until this thing is cleared up."

>>>

*So clear it up*, said Louisa Collins. *We need the video. You know that.*

The phone was feeling heavy in my hand. "Right, clear it up. Good. But exactly *what* am I supposed to be clearing up?"

*She's been dead five years, right? Why would somebody kill for a five-year-old video?*

"We don't know that somebody did."

*We don't know that somebody DIDN'T. What did he say? There's something sinister about the video? He's right. Find out why, and we've got what we need.*

Why did it sound so simple when she said it?

>>>

**THE PRE-LIFE**

They had space to give me my own office in the bureau. That was the one lone advantage of layoffs. Everybody was busy that morning microscoping through new and old photos of the actress Lee DaCosta. Pap shots taken last night seemed to show she'd had some surgery done. The distinctive bump on the bridge of Lee DaCosta's nose looked like it had been reduced. Was it the angle? A result of the flashes? The photos and her old ones were blown up for comparison. Didn't it seem smaller? A call was made to her publicist. No comment. We don't remark on our clients' body parts.

I stayed in my office. Time to start getting started.

I found a number for Robby Walsh's lobbying firm in Washington. They gave me another number to call, a

775 area code. Reno. I explained to the woman who answered that *Real Story* was looking into the Amanda Eston video and I wanted to talk to him about it. Could be off-the-record, background-only if he wanted.

I didn't get an outright rejection. Mr. Walsh is very busy. We'll try to schedule some time but we can't make any promises.

Of course not.

L.C. Martin was a different story. Yes, he'd meet me. Lunch today? Sure, he said. Absofuckinglutely.

>>>

I called up his bio files. They were much shorter than Amanda's.

•He grows up in blue-collar Ohio, the son of a pharmacist and a jewelry maker. The initials L.C. don't stand for anything. His birth certificate lists him as *L.C. Martin*. His father gets fired from several pharmacies because of chronic alcoholism. Finding work as a cab driver, he begins using heroin and develops a full-blown habit. L.C.'s mother sells jewelry on the streets to pay the bills.

•L.C. gets in fairly constant trouble, frequently suspended from school, arrested once—at 13—for auto theft. He often lives with his girlfriends and their families rather than his own home. At 16, he drops out of school and runs away to LA. "I hated school," he later says. "I hated every friggin' minute of it. It was hands-down, no-question the worst time of my life."

•He works illegally as a bouncer and occasional bartender in LA, though most of his time in the clubs is spent as a customer. In his dreams, he's determined to make it as…well, *something*, but he isn't sure what.

•A friend talks him into trying out for a new reality series, *The Pre-Life*, supposedly about a group of pre-med students surviving their first year in LA. L.C. gets cast on the strength of his looks and a smattering knowledge of medicine picked up from his father's years as a pharmacist.

•*The Pre-Life* premieres to dismal ratings and reviews. Critics question the show's authenticity, which is only natural since only a few cast members are actual pre-med students.

•"The producers were getting really desperate," L.C. later says, "so they began making changes. We began to appear with fewer and fewer clothes on. By the end of the first season, we were running around practically nude." The show turns into a hit, with L.C. recognized as the resident heartthrob.

•Weeks after the show finishes taping its second successful season, one of its stars, Rachel Newman, is killed in a car crash. The producers decide not to go on with a third season.

•Banking on his *Pre-Life* fame, L.C. gets himself cast in a few films. Neither they nor his career go anywhere.

•He auditions for a movie called *Days Of Reckoning*, starring Amanda Eston. To everyone's surprise, he gives an outstanding reading as her father, a role that requires him to age from a teen to an old man. The audition is no fluke: L.C.'s performance is hailed as a tour de force, touchingly truthful. He's named Best Supporting Actor by three critics' groups and wins an Oscar nomination in the same category.

•He marries Amanda. "I really thought I could help her with her addictions," he later says, "because of my experience with my father." They split after 11 turbulent months.

•While he's roundly urged to continue as a supporting actor, L.C. rejects the advice and keeps going after lead roles. The films flop and grow fewer and further apart.

•After organizing Amanda's funeral, L.C. wages a media campaign against Robby Walsh. The accusations keep him in the news for three or four months, then he begins to fade. He makes two more movies, both bad, and is never mentioned in the *Real Story* files again.

## UNFUCKINGDENIABLE

I did searches on him but couldn't find anything recent, couldn't find any reference to him after those last two loser movies. When we met for lunch, he told me he'd kissed acting goodbye. Now he was producing corporate videos—training sessions, sales pitches, orientation programs. Said he was doing very well with it.

He sure seemed prosperous. Gucci suit. Open Hilditch & Key dress shirt. Diamond-studded cufflinks. One of those pricey, octagonal-shaped, back-ordered-for-years Fleischer-Koch watches peaking out from under his French cuff.

L.C. looked the same as he did in his acting days. Older, but still quarterback handsome with a build to match. The only thing that felt different about him was his manner. He seemed twitchy and anxious.

He reminded me of a smoker who'd just
grabbed a few puffs and was now
experiencing some quivering, imperfect
nicotine buzz.

We met at Reggie's, on Robertson,
but well up the street from the pap-haunted
Ivy. He wanted to sit outside—"too many
ears indoors"—at a table away from
anybody else. We found one along the
white-washed arches that separated the
restaurant from the moneyed shoppers
strolling down the street.

A waitress wearing a tight
sleeveless T-shirt with a human stick
figure silkscreened on the front brought us
menus and took our drink orders. Diet
Coke for me, Stella Artois for him. I didn't
want to stare at the waitresses' chest, but
the head on the stick figure had a weird
but vague resemblance to those painted
faces I'd seen in Grady Alexander's

collection. Only this one was much more sophisticated, much more *produced*.

I've gotta stop free-associating in public.

L.C.'s first question: "Have you seen the whole video?"

"Just a couple more minutes."

I told him what it showed.

"This is so sad," he said. "This is so horribly sad. I know that's a cliché, I know it sounds a little exaggerated, but that's how it makes me feel."

Our drinks came. I sipped mine. He triple-sipped his.

"I guess there's one thing about the video," he said. "It's making people remember what happened. It's bringing her back."

"It's doing that."

"Unbelievable how people forget. Unbelievable how this amnesia fog falls over everything the second you look away. I mean, you know what I did, you know what I tried to do. I worked my bazoozies off trying to get people to look closer into what happened. But it just gets lost. It gets forgotten."

I shrugged. "Time passes."

"Yeah, time passes, sure it does. But not like that. Not at all like that."

He picked up his menu, eyes darting all over it like he'd seen it a million times. I studied mine.

Two women going inside Reggie's were talking to each other as they passed us by.

"Sex with him is such a pain in the ass," the one with the pink Dodgers cap was telling her friend. "And I mean that literally."

L.C. put his menu down. "People keep telling me, you gotta get on with your life. You gotta move on. Put it behind you. But how can you put it behind you when it's still fucking in front of you?"

"You still feel the same?"

"Same about what?"

"The official ruling."

"Fuck the ruling. Accidental overdose? Bullfuckingshit. What happened to her was no accident, and nobody but a knee-jerk idiot could believe it. The ruling, please. The ruling is positively, verifiably full of mistakes. All it is is *fart*-water and nothing more than that."

The waitress came back and took our order.

"I didn't start out like this," L.C. said when she was gone. "You know what it's like? You're looking at something everybody says is true, only the more you look at it you see it isn't true at all, it isn't

even close to true, only in your heart of
hearts you don't know what the fuck *is*
true?"

"But you found out."

"I *looked*. I looked at *everything*. I
looked at *pralicin*. Are you kidding me?
Pralicin? She never fucked around with
pralicin. Few people did—it was very
uncommon. The whole time I knew her,
she never even *mentioned* pralicin. And
even if she did it, even if she did it that
night, the evidence doesn't back it up."

"They found it in her system."

"But what *didn't* they find? That's
the question. Because with pralicin—I
looked into this—you swallow pralicin
capsules, you can tell. Pralicin capsules
leave a bluish purple discoloration on the
lining of the intestines."

I'm thinking, like *Purple Blues*, the
last movie she was going to make?

"But there wasn't any," he said. "I read the autopsy. I read it and read it and read it. There's no mention of any bluish purple discoloration. She didn't swallow any goddamn fistful of pralicin pills."

"So it got in another way."

"Somebody put it in her system. Somebody put a massive dose of it in her system. That's how they killed her. They killed the person I loved and that's how they did it. My whole life there was only one person I ever loved and *that's* how she died. They *killed* her."

He gulped his beer to a finish.

I let things sit. The tablecloth in front of us was beige with brown hairlike veins running through it.

"A question," I said. "Is that you in the video?"

L.C. laughed. "I don't have any birthmark on my cock. I can prove it to you. I'll pull it out right here."

"Not at lunchtime."

"No, it's not me. I hadn't seen her for a few days. If it's anybody, I think it's *him*."

"Robby Walsh?"

"Repulsive individual. Truly offensive. A scumbucket. He was with her all the time for a while there, *all* the time."

"Something tells me your opinion of him hasn't changed. You still think he killed her."

"Which is based on irrefutable thinking and stone-strong proof, which is based on proof so unfuckingdeniable it takes you to having no other opinion *but* that."

L.C. waved the waitress over, ordered another Artois and a shot of Jack Daniels.

"She wasn't stupid about things," he said. "People might think she was, but she wasn't. She read, she kept informed, she loved discussing things, she loved talking about politics. She was very interested in politics. *And, and* she was keeping a diary while she was seeing that halitoxic bastard. Or, not a diary—not an every day. A *journal*. She kept a journal on her computer. I think what was in there was what got her killed."

"You ever see it?

"No, it was her personal thoughts. But I know, you know, she *kept* it."

"How do you know?"

"She told me."

"You were that close?"

L.C. looked away from me, out to the street. "If you only knew."

His drinks came. He attacked the Jack, chased it with a third of the beer and told me how he and Amanda were getting back together.

No one was supposed to know it at the time. They didn't want to announce it until everything was settled. But they were reconciling, reconnecting. He'd realized he needed to be with her, he was lost without her. He said she was the best thing that had happened to him since he'd left his mama's womb.

And she felt the same way about him. She was tired of the loneliness, getting high all the time. He hadn't seen her in three, four days when she died, but they were definitely working things out between them, even thinking about getting remarried. She'd even bought a set of

dishes for a new house, was shopping for
bedroom furniture.

"What about Robby Walsh?"

"She was going to drop him," L.C.
said. "She was going to out-and-out dump
his ass. She said there were things about
him she didn't like."

"Like what?"

"She wouldn't say. It was
something she really didn't want to talk
about, but I think it was what he did time
for, the corruption, whatever else he had
locked in his shitbox. She wasn't like I
said stupid. I think she heard things,
picked things up, pillow talk, whatever. I
think that's what she had in her journal."

"What makes you think that?"

"I met a cop, a cop who was active
in the investigation. He told me the night
she died? They checked her computer.
They checked her computer right away.

There *was* no journal. It was gone. The thing disappeared the night she was killed."

"And you think Robby Walsh killed her to steal the journal."

"Probably not him himself. Probably some below-the-line people he hired. But for my money, yeah, he had the moral twerpitude to do it himself."

"You sure this isn't paranoia?"

"It's not paranoia if something actually happened."

Our food came. L.C. ordered a double Jack.

"You ever hear of Gerard Kimball?" he said. "Sgt. Gerard Kimball?"

"No."

"He was the first LAPD officer to respond to her house. Bodyguard let him in, took him to the bedroom. He sees her sprawled facedown, naked, laying diagonally across the bed. Reports it in. So on and so on.

"Few days later he runs into this photographer he knows, a paparazzo. Guy says to Gerard, I've got to tell you about something, but it's totally in confidence. Gerard agrees. The photographer says that on the night she died, he got a call from this German magazine—magazine, website, whatever—he'd done work for before. This was a little after 11 that night, 11:15 the latest. They told him to get over to Amanda Eston's house—she's dead and they want him to shoot the story for them. He went, but by the time he got there the cops were all over the place. Except for the outside of the house, he couldn't get any footage.

"Next day, though, the photographer reads that the bodyguard didn't find her until 11:47. So how—this

is what he tells Gerard—how did this
German magazine know she was dead at
11:15 the latest, a good half-hour before?"

"Who was the photographer?

"Gerard never told me the name. It
was in confidence."

"So what did this Gerard do?"

While we picked at our food, L.C.
told me what happened next.

>>>

Sgt. Gerard Kimball is completely twisted
by the discrepancy in time. He presses the
photographer on the hour. You sure it
wasn't after 12? No, the guy remembers
watching *The Daily Show* live when he got
the call—it had to be after 11. The guy's
also reluctant to give up the name of the
German magazine, website, whatever. He
doesn't want to jeopardize an income

source. But eventually he tells. Gerard finds out that the Germans got a call from an anonymous tipster just after 11 p.m. Pacific time, simply telling them that Amanda Eston had died. They aren't able to trace the call back.

Gerard starts questioning what's going on, a process that will turn out to be long and tortuous.

•Her remembers seeing her body, facedown, positioned diagonally across the bed, remembers seeing her right hand outstretched toward the cell phone on her nightstand. Like she was struggling, at the end, to make or take a call. He looks in the reports for her phone records, discovers that the FBI has already tracked all calls in and out that night. The last calls she made include two to Robby Walsh's cell, one to his office, one to his house. Two calls came in, both from Walsh's cell.

•Maybe a week later, Gerard starts thinking he should make copies of the phone records for future reference. But when he goes back, they're missing. Long-distance calls, the LUDS—they've just up and disappeared from the records. And nobody can say what happened. Huh? Gerard spends weeks trying to run them down, even calls the FBI, but nobody knows nothing. The records are officially lost.

•A while later he makes a contact in the ME's office. The woman in question tells him that Amanda's body was in an advanced state of rigor mortis when it arrived at the hospital. Meaning she'd been dead for several hours, much earlier than the estimated TOD noted in the autopsy. Gerard is never able to nail this down, but in the course of asking he finds there's a widespread rumor running through the department. Allegedly, the ME refused to sign off on the accidental-overdose ruling, but was pressured into it by his superiors.

•Trying to put the patterns and links together, Gerard gets in touch with L.C. L.C. tells him about the missing journal. Gerard remembers the techies going through her computer at the scene. That's *exactly* what they were looking for, something personal like a journal, but they couldn't find a thing. Gerard double-checks the old tech reports. No journal was ever located.

•He starts going rogue, telling people in the media that the official ruling is bogus and that Amanda's body should be exhumed and reexamined. LAPD brass tells him to shut the fuck up.

•Gerard eventually comes up with a theory about what happened that night.

Someone who knew Amanda, someone who had the keys to her house and who knew the alarm codes, had duplicate keys made. The keys and the code were given to someone else, possibly more than one person. That person or persons let themselves in the house that night, probably making sure she was asleep first. They held her down and inserted a pralicine enema in her rectum. Ingested in this manner, the drug works quickly. She would have struggled for only a minute, then gotten woozy as her breathing slowed. Her breathing would gradually decrease over the next 12-15 minutes, at which point she would be dead. This would allow plenty of time for the computer to be hacked and her journal removed. Then the intruder or intruders would exit, reset the alarm and lock the front door, leaving no evidence of a break-in. Amanda might still have a minute or so, just before she died, to try to use the phone.

>>>

The afternoon sun was turning the ground into an oven. Traffic was stalling on Robertson, getting heavy. I saw a white refrigerated truck crawl past. NOBODY BEATS OUR MEAT.

"I'd like to talk to Gerard Kimball. You know where he is?"

"One of two places," said L.C. "He called a press conference on his own, unauthorized. He was demanding, you can guess, that the investigation be formally reopened. I was there. I saw it. Gerard walked up to the microphones, started talking about the gaps in the official ruling, the unanswered questions. About a minute into it, he coughed once—just once, one single cough—then he collapsed to the floor and stopped breathing. Everybody started running and screaming. There were, I don't know, three or four people trying to give him CPR, which maybe wasn't such a good thing. Any case, by the time the EMTs got there, he was dead. Huge heart attack. Monumental heart attack, although he'd never had any heart problems. No history whatsoever."

I waited a beat, waited for it.

"You're saying somebody killed him? You're saying Robby Walsh killed him too?"

L.C. gave a sisyphus shrug. "I can't prove a thing. I don't know what that anger-banger did to Gerard. But sure as shit I know what he did to her. I know and I will never forgive. I know what that clammy scumbag did and I will never forget, and I know that someday somebody's gonna cut through all this froo-frah-frah and make somebody tell the fucking *truth*."

"It could happen."

"And if not me—I ask you this—if not me, then who the fuck *who*? That's why it'll be me. They haven't killed my energy—my energy is very, very big. I *will* do it. And when I say I, I means *me*."

Well, his energy might've been very, very big, but it suddenly seemed to drop off. He started staring at his empty Jack Daniels tumbler and he didn't move. He was staring at the glass as if it had hypnotized him.

"You okay?"

"I'm okay," he said slowly. "Just, sometimes, I get depressed by all this. Sometimes I think about what a disaster my life is since she's been gone, how fuckered-up everything is. Sometimes I feel like I got electrodes stuck to my head, and these thoughts are being run through the night and into my skull, and once they get in there they start dilating and bloating until it feels like my head is going to crack open. I'm trying to do this, I'm trying to do this for her, sometimes I get so depressed light stops moving. I can see it. I can see the light molecules just slow down and stop moving."

The way L.C. was talking, the way he looked, he reminded me of a guy I'd once done a story on, a guy who was suing the state to get back *into* prison. Claimed his release was illegal, granted on faulty grounds, and should be reversed. Life outside was so bad, he said, he was desperate to get back inside.

"I know you loved her," I said, "I know what you're trying to do, but you can't let it warp your life."

L.C. laughed. "That's what they all say. That's what a lot of people say. But you know what? Show me somebody who's gone through what I've gone through, who's got the same ghosts I have, who's pushed his thoughts to the edge, whose thoughts are splitting his fucking head apart, whose life has been turned into an utter fucking ruin, who's lost without the person he loves, who loved somebody who had people leeching off her soul, who loved somebody who got ravaged and devoured and luminously chewed apart, and if he's got the exact same loss that I have, the *exact* same, pound for pound, pain for pain, measure for measure, then let him tell me... Ah, shit, what am I talking about? I don't know what the fuck I'm talking about."

His eyes lost their focus. He hunched over the table and lowered his head.

"I don't know what I'm doing sometimes," he said. "You know? I just don't know what I'm doing."

"You're sitting here. You're having lunch with me."

He nodded. He moved his head with the force of revelation. "Right, right. I'm sitting here. I'm having lunch with you."

>>>

## BLACK PATENT LEATHER
## LACE-UP BOOTS

I went back to the bureau, did some catch-up work. It helped me come down from L.C., absorb what he'd said. Later I had dinner with the bureau chief, JoEllen Sanchez. She wanted to talk about language, the way people sterilize and denude it these days. Especially the bureaucrats who run our company.

"It just spins my head off," JoEllen said. "A vacation is now an Extended Out-Of-Office Leave. An EOOOL. Overtime? An Accelerated Pro-Rated Incremental Payment. An APRIP."

She was right. Where does it end? Bums don't pick up butts on the street anymore? They pick up pre-smoked cigarettes? PSCs?

There was a message waiting for me back at the Chateau Marmont. The concierge handed me a hotel envelope, one of those old pink While-U-Where-Out slips. From: L.C. Martin. Message: *Please meet him at his house. He has something to show you.* Address: 317 Emory Road, in Santa Monica.

Well why not? You can never get enough L.C. Martin in one day.

I drove, thinking about a story I'd read recently. A gang of teens had gone wild in Santa Monica, driving through the streets and shooting up cars. But only expensive cars—Bentleys, Jaguars, BMWs. If you had a KIA, you were safe.

No, there's no class warfare in America.

I found Emory Road, no problem, but the street confused me. It was a commercial drag. Nothing remotely residential about it. I saw tall buildings up ahead. Maybe L.C. lived in a condo? But the semi-scrapers turned out to be office buildings. No condos, co-ops or apartments. Just blocks of quiet, almost deserted darkness.

Did whoever took the message get it wrong? Or was L.C. so far gone he couldn't remember where he lived?

There wasn't even a 317 Emory Road. You had an office building at 315 and another at 319. Between them was the entrance to an open parking lot in the back.

That's where 317 should've been, right there. A neat non-existent fit.

*Very* neat, in fact. It almost felt on-purpose.

I'm thinking, is this really a mistake? Or does crazy L.C. want me to see something in there?

I pulled in. What the hell, I was already here. The parking lot, fenced in its back, spanned the two buildings. It had three entrances, the one I was using, the others running down the far sides of 315 and 319. Fifteen or 16 cars were scattered throughout, lit by the empty pink glow of sodium vapor lights.

Could L.C. be waiting for me in one of the parked cars? I drove around the lot, scouted them out. Nobody inside any of them. Nothing here except a kind of jumpy static in the night.

I looked at the two office buildings. Something in there? I parked my car and closed the door softly as I got out, I don't know why, but it was like I didn't want to disturb the atmosphere. There were a few lights on in each building, people working late. These are their cars.

I started walking toward the closest building, 319, and halfway there I heard the sound of running in the middle entrance, the one I'd used. No, *feet* running, more than one person, voices, thick, the sounds echoing between the buildings.

A Suburu Forester was parked 12 feet away from me. I ducked behind the side of the car, staying down enough to keep my eyes just above the lower edge of the windows.

Two guys ran into the lot. Big guys, mostly meat. Each had what looked like a gun in his hand, each had his face covered with a gaily multicolored ski mask.

Nah—no way this could be good.

They stood for a second in the lot, then one of them said, "That's him," and they started running again. To the rental I was driving.

Still crouching next to the Suburu, I took the Glock out.

They looked at my rental, circled it, checked the inside, then looked up and around the rest of the lot.

"Shit," one of them said. "That way."

"No," said the other. "*That* way."

They started moving toward 319, coming *this* way. I dropped to the ground and rolled under the Suburu. Better dirty than dead.

All I could see now were their feet. One guy was wearing grubby work shoes. But the other, Jesus, he had on a pair of black patent leather lace-up boots, the surface gleaming in the pink parking lights.

Where do you even *buy* these things?

They went past the Suburu and over to 319, not going near the door but hugging close to the shadows by the wall. I saw them turn down the car entranceway on the far side of the building, heard their steps fade away as they ran toward the street.

I didn't move. I must've breathed but I don't remember. Two entire minutes passed. No steps, no sounds, no movement in the shadows.

I rolled out from underneath the Suburu and got to my feet. I was definitely getting that Robert Johnson feeling—time to move on, time to outrace the devil.

Twenty feet from my rental I heard a harsh heel-scrape in the middle alley. My pulse jumped to my temples. A figure edged out of those shadows. He was shorter than the other guys. Squat, powerful build, also with a ski mask—

slashes and diagonals of reds, yellows and blues—covering his face.

I didn't notice what shoes he was wearing because he had a gun in his hand big enough to cut a Lincoln Tunnel through my head.

Total panic. A shit-volley of shots blew out as I ran, bullets spitting up cement splinters all around my legs. I dove for the rental and leveled my Glock on the hood. One shot. It caught him in the shoulder, spun him around and knocked him to the ground.

I'd like to know who he was but the circumstances for an introduction didn't seem right.

I gunned the rental across the lot and swung into the alley on the far side of 315. Clear going for maybe three seconds until the first two ski-masked guys suddenly materialized in front of me,

running in from the street. They saw me
and raised their guns. I plowed straight at
them, ramming the rental up another 40 or
50 miles per hour.

They went blind as they jumped
out of the way, throwing themselves into a
random choreography of arms, legs, wild
air-shots and black patent leather lace-up
boots.

>>>

I drove back to the Chateau asking
myself—all the way—what I thought was
a pretty natural question. WHAT THE
FUCK WAS THAT? How had that
happened? Had L.C. set me up? I went to
call him—I had his number from when I
first called for the meet. But instead I
called Kumiko Davis in New York. Could
she run a quick check on L.C. Martin's

home address? Did he live in Santa
Monica, anywhere near the vicinity of
Emory Road?

It took her two minutes. No,
nowhere near there. His address was 58
Chenille Lane, Beverly Glen.

I called L.C.

"Did you leave a message for me at
my hotel?"

*What're you TALKING about?*

I told him. He went off like a
nuclear warhead.

*You SEE? You see the SCOPE of
it, the dimensions? They're after you.
That's how wide this thing is, that's the
REACH of it. They're after you now.*

"Who? Robby Walsh?"

*You go careful with him. You go
careful with him and those people. They're
dangerous. They're CORRUPTING. You*

*deal with them you end up talking like a Republican and sleeping with prostitutes.*

"Sorry?"

*Bottom line, what I'm saying here is, there's no TRUTH. NOBODY'S telling any motherfucking TRUTH. And you know why? Cause it's DANGEROUS. Things are dangerous. We live in dangerous times.*

An echo of Arnoud Shuyler.

"But haven't people been saying that," I said, "since we started keeping time?"

>>>

Should I report the shoot-out to the police? Probably not. My chances of buying the video from Grady Alexander, I thought, would get appreciably dimmer if I did. No matter how much Grady talked about the legality of his head candy, I didn't think he'd be open to a deal that had cops hanging all over it. And with guns going off in the streets? On top of Arnoud Shuyler's death? No, Grady would shut down like a catatonic on smack. So I wouldn't go to the cops. Not yet.

>>>

I checked out of the Chateau Marmont that night and checked into the Four Seasons. Under a different name.

>>>

# >>>CHAPTER 3

## >>EYES OF RAZORS AND BLOOD

**SOME VERY WEIRD WAVELENGTHS**

Another message. I got it the next morning. This one came in through the *Real Story* bureau's general number, and after the usual series of human and technological delays eventually got transferred to the office I was using. Another message, but this one felt different. It was from Tasha Eston, Amanda's sister. L.C. had told her I was in town, asking about Amanda's death.

I called the number she'd left.

*I hear you met L.C. yesterday, had a long talk.*

"We did."

*I think I'd better talk to you.*

Tasha suggested lunch. Okay with me, but can we make it a more out-of-the-way place than Reggie's? She knew the perfect spot: Café St. Anthony's.

To meet its expenses and keep its funding going, St. Anthony's Church, right nearby in Westwood, had converted its terrace into an open-air restaurant. Nice joint—a little piece of secluded, friendly, sun-dappled paradise.

Tasha looked a lot like her sister. No mole, but her lips were definitely Estonesque. Same plump, witchy sultriness. Her eyes were different, though. Amanda's had been large and almondy and strangely peaceful. Tasha's were smaller and maybe not model-perfect, but the at-peace expression was way more pronounced.

We sat at a table for two, surrounded by other lunchers. She was wearing carefully crumpled jeans, a crisp white shirt, a small gold cross around her neck and a pair of shades resting on top of her head. Strong whiff of allspice and cloves to her, maybe as a result of what she did for a living. She was a rep for what she called a comprehensive line of organic soap, cosmetic and hair-care products.

"Did you hear about broccoli?" someone at one of the near tables said. "Did you hear what they say?"

I didn't care, not today.

"So you thought I should talk to you."

Tasha laughed. "After a dose of L.C.? Yeah, I thought it was called for. Me, I can't do it anymore. I can't listen to anymore of him. It's all, this is the way

things would've happened if they
would've happened this way."

"You think he's off the wall?"

"Don't misunderstand, I love L.C.
Just that sometimes he gets a
little…inconsequential. Sometimes he gets
wired into some very weird wavelengths."

"So you don't believe what he
says."

"I'm a big disbeliever in what he
says. What L.C. is, he's a crumb-gobbler.
He'll pick up little pieces of this, little
pieces of that, try to mush them together
into one big cookie. But the cookie keeps
crumbling apart."

"I don't know, he brings up some
interesting questions."

"There are always questions in
things like this, like what happened. Any
trip to the hospital, somebody forgets
something, somebody doesn't know,

something gets misplaced, your records don't get switched over. Happens."

"And the rest of it? All that Robby Walsh stuff?"

"Please, L.C. and Robby Walsh. Whose wiener is meaner. I'm sick of it."

We ordered. She got a red-oak lettuce salad with tangerine wedges, mint sprigs, toasted pignolis and ricotta salada. I went for the butternut squash ravioli with Marion County blackberries. Funny thing, I couldn't remember what I ate with L.C., and that was only yesterday. This food, I remembered every bite.

"What you're saying," I said as the menus were carried away, "you're okay with the official ruling. Accidental overdose?"

"No."

"No?"

"Overdose, yes. Accidental, no. She did it on purpose. Sad thing is, she didn't think she could help it."

"Can't help killing yourself?"

"She talked about the family history, not fighting it, playing out the Eston family legacy."

"What legacy is that?"

"We come from a long line of self-killers."

"Suicides tend to run in families."

"Thirteen in 27 years? That's a big statistical chunk."

"Thirteen? No exaggeration?"

"Not by one."

Jesus Christ and his brother Bob.

"Well, I know about your father and mother."

Tasha took the sunglasses off her head and laid them on the table.

"I don't remember my father much, I was just a year old when he left. What I can remember is a man with dark circles under his eyes, that's about it. And I can remember the smell of his aftershave. Strange thing to remember."

"Those things happen."

"We never saw him after he left. Then one day, I was 3, all of a sudden there's a lot of people in our house. I knew something had happened to him. Later I found out he'd been living in a rooming house up in D.C., an SRO. They found him in his bed, sheet soaked in blood. He'd slashed his own throat."

"I'm sorry. Bad thing to learn."

Tasha played with her glasses. "My mother always said they fought a lot. She'd say that when he got mad, you could see the razors and blood in his eyes. She never knew how prophetic she was."

Living out in semi-suburban
Virginia, she said, there wasn't much in
the way of counseling after suicides. A
shame, because she thought her mother at
least could've used some. Her mother
started to get real fruity, or even more so,
after her father died. Hands trembling,
crying all the time, talking trash about her
own children. She never should've had
Amanda, she told both kids, *I should've
blown him instead.* As for Tasha, she
admitted she'd tried to miscarry her by
drinking quinine. She said she wasn't
ready for children—she was under too
much stress.

Which is why—for a time—the
girls kept getting residentially toggle-
switched, out of the house with other
relatives, back in the house with mom. It
was the other relatives who enrolled

Amanda in acting, singing and dancing classes.

Tasha was 7, Amanda 9, when their mother was finally sent away. The girls were told she was going to live in a home for sad people, and Tasha had no reason to believe it wasn't true. When they went to visit, she always seemed unhappy and unhealthy. Even news about Amanda's St. Joseph's Aspirin commercial, or getting voice work in cartoons, couldn't cut through the sadness. Their mother would complain that she couldn't sleep, couldn't eat, though everyone else would say, *no, she's getting better, she's doing much better.*

"I was at school one afternoon, a policewoman walked into the class, asking for me. She took me into the hall, said something had happened and she had to take me back to my Aunt Renee's. The whole drive I was thinking my sister or my aunt had been involved in some kind of accident. I couldn't even ask the policewoman a question I was so scared. Then she pulled into my aunt's driveway and took me inside. Amanda was sitting on the couch. Aunt Renee too, arm around her. They were both crying, *sobbing*. That's when I knew—it was my mother. They'd moved her to a halfway house and she'd hung herself in the women's bathroom, tied a bedsheet around one of the ceiling supports in the stall."

>>>

The food arrived. We dug into it like it was the bread of life. Tasha ate with a good appetite, despite what she was talking about, despite compiling the Eston family body count.

She used to think the pattern had started with her father, but as she grew up she found about the other blood deaths. It was like suicide was coded in the family DNA.

•Her uncle, her father's brother, had killed himself with their father's snub-nosed .38 handgun.

•One of her grandfathers had driven his car off a bridge.

•One of her grandmother's sisters on the other side of the family had starved herself to death. Five-foot-three and 48 pounds when she died.

•A cousin, only 12 years old, had taken a hatchet to his house, chopped up all the furniture, smashed all the windows, then put a 12-gauge shotgun in his mouth as the police responded.

•An older cousin walked in to her son's bedroom one night, put a gun to the sleeping boy's head and fired once before turning the gun on herself.

•One of Aunt Renee's own sons had gone to the top floor of the tallest building in Richmond, thrown a chair through a plate-glass window and jumped.

•Among other relatives, there were two overdoses, two slashed wrists and one death by carbon monoxide poisoning when an aunt left her car exhaust running in a locked garage.

Thirteen in 27 years.

Loss after loss after loss.

>>>

"We're really lucky, you know," someone at one of the other tables was saying. "We're lucky to be living in the Milky Way."

All things considered, we probably were.

"Amanda knew all this, right?" I said. "She talked about it?"

"All the time. She thought a lot about joining the rest of the family, fulfilling the family heritage, the destiny. She'd try to keep busy with other things, but it was always there, the thing under the other things. She could always feel the past reaching out for her."

"Always? All through school and everything?"

"That I don't know. School I don't know. We weren't so close growing up. It was only later, when I came out here, that we got to be friends."

"Is that why you moved here?"

Tasha shook her head like she was flinging shower water out of her hair. "That was the producers' idea. She'd just held up a movie, *Call And Response*, and they didn't want to go through it again. They thought, get a family member out here, maybe she'll simmer down some. The producers paid for my move, got me enrolled mid-semester in marketing courses, UCLA. That's when I got to know her."

"And she talked about the family history?"

"She talked about the fear, the old terrors that come at you in the night. She talked a lot about it toward the end, what turned out to be the end. She thought suicide was like this big goddamn magnet that just swooped us all to it."

"At the end, toward the end, she talk at all about Robby Walsh?"

She shrugged the subject away. "They were seeing each other—she told me about that. She liked him—it was new thing, you know?—but it wasn't too serious."

"She talk about bribes, pay-offs?"

"Never."

"What about L.C.? Were they really getting back together?"

"I don't know—it was vague. It was *very* vague."

"She bought dishes? Went shopping for furniture?"

"She was *always* shopping, always buying something. I know what L.C. thinks, but that's only in the look-back. It wasn't like that when it was happening."

"He has an odd form of nostalgia?"

"*Very.*"

"And you? How do you look back on it?"

Tasha had one tangerine wedge left in her dish. She stared at it for a while, then speared it and ate it.

"With regret," she said. "I'm sorry I wasn't there. I'm sorry I wasn't with her that night."

"Did you stay over often?"

"Never. She liked her privacy. Even when I moved she wouldn't let me stay with her, but we talked almost every day. The only time I really stayed there was when that guy was bothering her, and that was only for a week or two. Otherwise, she liked to keep a guard on, what did she call it, her *personal* self."

I glanced around us. Beautiful setting. Blue and yellow light hanging over the Westwood horizon.

"A guy was bothering her?"

"A stalker. She had lots of stalkers, goes with the territory, but this one… She really went tailspinny over this one, asked me to stay over. Said she was scared to death—that's what she said when she testified against him."

How had I missed this in the files? I'd just skipped it over?

"Who was he?"

"Some homeless black guy. African-American. He started showing up everywhere, on location, following her to parties. Sent her hundreds of notes. They even caught him sleeping on her property once. She went to a premiere one night, he stood outside the theater and took all his clothes off, yelling at her please save me, please save me. Then he got violent with the security people."

"What happened?

"He got arrested, went to jail. He was mad-crazy."

"When was this?"

"Long time ago. A couple of years before she died."

"Is he still in jail?"

"I have no idea. I haven't thought about him in years. I never thought of him as a factor in what happened, if that's where you're going. And I still don't."

"Family history."

"She thought she was helpless against it. She thought no matter what she did, she couldn't get away."

"I know. You climb and climb and climb, but there's always something downstairs."

Tasha took a long breath, picked up her glasses and fixed them on her head. "Growing up's a bitch, it really is."

"Nothing leaves you less prepared to be an adult than childhood."

She nodded, moved her head for a long time. Too long for just a response—

something was on her mind. "If you find anything out, will you let me know?"

**HAUNTED FACES**

This time when I went through Amanda's bio-files, I narrowed the search to *stalking*. That's how I figured out why I hadn't seen it before. She hadn't testified at the trial— when she said she was scared to death, she'd only given a taped deposition. She'd never gone to the courthouse. That's why there were no photo tags, no video, only a few tiny storylets. It wasn't a media event.

I'd only been looking for the highlights of her life my first time around. This wasn't considered big news.

But it went the way Tasha said. Whether Amanda was working, partying or sleeping, the guy followed her around like heat on fire. He once tried to break into her trailer on a shoot. He mailed letters, sometimes three or four a day, confessing that he was obsessively in love with her. Many of the letters were accompanied by strange and disturbing drawings. When he stripped down naked at the premiere and asked her to save him, he threatened to kill the guards restraining him. And when they found a box-cutter in his pants pocket, they called the cops.

His name was Norridge Morris.

Of course I knew who he was. Grady Alexander had bought his belongings at a public storage auction. Grady had found the video of her last night in Norridge Morris' junk.

A jury convicted Norridge on two counts of second-degree aggravated harassment and two counts of fourth-degree stalking. At his sentencing hearing, where he was given two years, he made a point of telling the court that he wasn't at all angry at Amanda and still loved her very much.

He served 16 months and was released five years ago. He was released 10 days before Amanda Eston was found dead.

>>>

I asked the bureau chief, JoEllen Sanchez, for help. How do I track down a homeless person, or possibly a former homeless person? She suggested various agencies—Bring LA Home, the Los Angeles Homeless Services Authority, the Shelters Resource Bank, LA's Homeless Blog, church groups—and said things would go better if I knew the person's real and full name.

I said I did. "Norridge Morris."

JoEllen looked at me. "*Norridge* Morris?"

"Norridge Morris."

She started laughing like I was one of the bigger idiots ever put on this earth. "You don't know much about fashion, do you?"

>>>

Turns out Norridge Morris was one of the great success stories on the LA—and now national—clothing-design scene. Three, almost four years ago, a pair of local entrepreneurial-minded young guys began noticing Morris on the streets. He always slept in the same alley, always wore capes and hoodies and T-shirts painted with these bizarre faces. The two guys, Jake Kaufman and Bobby Rubin, were really taken by the faces. Unique. Tribal. Haunted. They told Norridge, when he was lucid, they were looking to start a fashion line, and they thought his faces would be cool on women's clothes.

It took the guys nearly half a year of talking to gain Norridge's trust, but eventually they did. The called the label Crazy Face, and Norridge, the third partner, began turning out whole troops of new faces.

They placed their first order at Kitson's main boutique on Robertson. Fifteen T-shirts, five hoodies. Gone in one day. Kitson's reordered. Forty T-shirts, 25 hoodies, one cape. Gone, gone, gone.

By now Crazy Face had its own trademarked logo and was selling wildly in chains all over the country. Hell, even I unknowingly noticed it. The waitress at Reggie's with the stick figure T-shirt? That was a Crazy Face.

>>>

## STUPORSTITIONS

The label's offices were located in downtown LA, near the Walt Disney Concert Hall. When I called, Norridge said he was really busy, but when I told him the Amanda Eston video going around had been found in his stuff, he decided he could squeeze me in.

I found a parking garage and walked a block to the building. A guy with a sandwich board was picketing in front of the entrance. He had a scraggly, toxic mustache and an Oakland Raiders cap propped on top of a sweatband. According to his sign, three unions were calling for a boycott of Crazy Face because the company was refusing to negotiate over benefits.

Pretty ironic. In the space of a few years, Norridge Morris had gone from being homeless to being picketed.

In America, this is known as a *win*.

Crazy Face had its headquarters in a fourth-floor loft big enough to hold 18 or 20 bowling lanes. A few staffers were talking to each other in the reception area. "Ronald Reagan? Ronald *Reagan*? You're saying Ronald Reagan was *gay*?" A well-dressed woman with a black eyepatch took me to Norridge's window-walled space.

He was a gracious, courtly gentleman with a lion's mane of long gray hair, wearing pressed khakis and a Crazy Face T-shirt. His voice was street-graveled but deliberately formal, like he was on the verge of bowing each time he spoke.

Three women wearing jeweled flip-flops and not a whole hell of a lot else were in conference with Norridge.

"Ladies," he said, "would you kindly give us a moment?"

A man of old-fashioned manners, who still called women ladies.

When we were alone I told him more about the video. I said that a collector—no names—had bought his leftovers at a storage auction. The inventory included early Crazy Face prototypes, foreign currency, a flask and a disk.

"I confess, I'm boggled," Norridge said in his soft croak. "The whole thing just boggles me."

"You remember the disk?"

"I barely do. That whole time in my life is one bad blur. I remember...I remember my *extreme* interest in Amanda Eston, yes, of course, but my life then was one stinkfish blur."

"You remember how your interest started?"

"I had no idea who she was. Some big actress. She was hosting this charity event, raising money for street people. They were giving out free food. That's why I went. That's the first time I saw her."

"That's when it happened?"

"It was like being swept up in a windstorm. I was…I was *possessed*. I was head-to-foot *possessed*. The things I did. I was spinning in a storm to do the things I did."

"Letters, threats."

"Arrest." Norridge looked at me, 4,000 memories running through his eyes. "I paid my price."

"What happened when you got out?"

"I promised myself I would leave her alone. I bore no animosity toward her. I told myself it wouldn't be right to bother

her. Then I heard she'd died. Little over a week after my release. I heard she'd died and I felt like I'd died too. I was broken all to pieces, started drinking heavy again."

"And?"

"I promised myself I wouldn't go near her or her place again. But after she died, I *had* to. I had to make one last visit. I went by the house a few days after, it was night. Place was cop-taped off, padlock on the door. But there was trash bags out in back. Somebody I guess had cleaned out the nonessentials and dumped them in the back. I went through it. Mostly Weight Watchers boxes, spoiled food. But there was this disk. In a case. I didn't know what it was, some music I thought, but I figured maybe it meant something to her, so I kept it."

"You never looked at it?"

"Man, I had no computer. I had nothing to play it on. I just kept it. Then…then it all went pretty quick after that. I got pretty booze-fucked after that. Maybe I put it in storage. I was putting things in storage back then, but I don't remember what. All I can remember from those years is one thing. I loved her. Even today, telling you the truth, I still love her."

The woman with the eyepatch came in—sorry to interrupt, but we need a sign-off on these right away. She spread a dozen promotional photos of Norridge on his desk.

He perused, head going back and forth. "I'm sorry, darling," he said like gravel slowly falling from a dump truck. "I'm afraid I have to say no."

"What's wrong?"

"Look how I look. I'm all...*puffy*. And that smile. That wet-noodle smile. What's with that, that *fake*-noodle smile?"

"You wanna see more?"

"Or else schedule a reshoot. I'm sorry, these won't do."

She scooped up the photos and left.

My brilliant observation: "You've done all right for yourself."

No argument from Norridge. "When Jake and Bobby found me, I had nothing. Had a total of two dollars in my pocket, only because somebody had paid it back to me after a month's time. I was totally skint. But they helped me. They got me into AA."

"I know Bill myself."

"Then you know."

"I know you can walk in there with a lot of stuporstitions in your head."

"Yes, indeed. But those guys… You know, I signed a contract with them, never even consulted a lawyer? I tell that to people, they look at me. But those boys never did me wrong."

"I hear sales're good."

"Flying off the proverbial shelves. Plus we're branching out. Hats, handbags. And *this*."

He reached into a drawer, produced a cell phone with one of his faces embossed on the top.

"Fantastic brand extension," he said. "Comes with a prepaid phone card, 100 free minutes."

"Very nice."

"Take it. Have one."

"I can't."

"It's good to go."

"Company policy—I can't accept gifts."

"It's not a *gift*. Give me a dollar, we'll call it even."

>>>

## A BAD PLACE TO BE

The protestor with the sandwich board and the Raiders hat was still outside the building, steadily mumbling to himself like he was saying the rosary without the beads. I did a little mumbling myself as I walked back to the parking garage. How much of Norridge's story could I buy? Probably a hefty slice of it. I was willing to believe much of what he said, willing to believe he had nothing to do with her death. I just wished there was more left to his memory. I wished there was a stronger chain of evidence between him finding the video and the video ending up in Grady Alexander's hands.

No matter what, though, his story pointed out the fundamental insanity of the situation. I was trying to bid $12 or $15 million for something somebody had tossed in the trash.

I was maybe 100 feet inside the parking garage, fumbling in my pocket, making sure I had my ticket, when I heard the noise behind me. A thumping, a rhythmic smacking, like somebody was banging on something hard like wood.

I turned around and saw the protestor in the garage's lunar light. Oakland cap, fungusy mustache. He was running behind me, knees knocking against his sandwich board.

What the hell is *his* problem?

I found out. He pulled a gun from under his board, raised it in my direction and took a running shot.

A hundred square feet of rear-window glass blew out of the Honda S2000 next to me.

What did I do, cross a picket line?

I dove to the front of the S2000, ducked between its grill and the garage wall and reached for my Glock. His sandwich board made a beautiful target. I hit it twice, sending him staggering backward. He bounced off a parked Buick Lucerne and stumbled for cover behind a cement column.

Then it was quiet.

"What the hell *is* this?" I yelled.

"What do you *think*?"

"No fucking idea."

"You know what we want."

"What? What d'you want?"

"No fucking around. You *know* what we want."

"I don't. And who the fuck is *we*?"

He answered with a staccato burst of gunfire. Very articulate.

Quiet again.

I waited, tense, watching. Long as he stayed in the shadows behind the column I wasn't getting a shot.

I saw a big Yukon Denali two cars over from me. Good cover, better angle. I stood in a crouch, started firing at him and scrambled over to the Yukon, my shots echoing off every surface of garage cement.

I let a few seconds pass, then began crawling to the other end of the Yukon. From there, I thought, I'd get a good perspective on the guy.

I'd just reached the rear fender when a blast of gunfire behind me riddled the Yukon and made all the garage walls billow gray.

I jumped back to the front of the Yukon and looked. An insanely ugly guy had just come running around a corner of the garage. He had two rows of hair rutting back across a shaved head. Looked like tire tracks on his skull.

He kept firing at me from the shadows—it was like being shot at by antimatter—until he disappeared behind a column.

This was a bad place to be. I frog-jogged back to the S2000 and ducked down. The protestor began shooting at me. The tire-track guy began shooting at me. Together they were setting off 468 echoes in the garage. You couldn't hear God scream in that noise.

They had me triangulated. They had me trapped.

Finally, a lull. They were waiting, looking to see what comes next. I took the Crazy Face phone out of my pocket, found its number and laid it on the ground in front of the S2000.

"Okay," I yelled. "Okay. I have what you want."

"Glad to hear it," said the protestor.

"Let's talk."

"Just slide the gun out."

"Not a fucking chance. We'll talk on even terms."

The protestor thought about it. "Two to one isn't even."

"I'll take it."

I stood up, slowly came out from behind the S2000. They stepped away from their respective columns. Each had his gun trained on me. I switched mine between them, my cell hidden in my other fist.

"Just come steady," said the protestor. "Come ahead."

I walked carefully out into the open, putting distance between myself and the S2000.

"That's far enough."

Probably was. I pressed the button on my cell.

*So much darkness in the world these days, you know?*

It was Arnoud Shuyler's taped voice, playing on my cell but coming through a call to the Crazy Face phone, volume turned to high.

*Darkness all around, Mr. McShane. All around.*

They were confused. They shifted their heads to the S2000.

*So much darkness these days some people can't even see it.*

I shot the protestor in the shin, just below the sandwich board. He fell to the floor screaming in pain.

*So much darkness they think they're still looking at the light.*

The tire-track guy took a wild shot at me. I hammered him with a bullet to his ribs.

Neither would stay down forever. I ran for my rental. I was gone faster than the Times Square clean-up after New Year's Eve.

>>>

I once knew a boxer, or ex-boxer, who told me about his last fight. He thought he was holding his own until the end of the sixth round. "I went back to the corner," he said, "my own cut man passed out from the sight of my blood. That's when I knew how bad I getting beaten."

I was starting to understand *exactly* how he felt.

>>>

# >>>CHAPTER 4

## >>UNOBLITERATED

### UNDER THE MOUNTAIN

My life has become an obsessive search for messages. You send an idea out, then you wait and keep looking through your email and text messages and call logs for a response. Has anyone seen it yet? Has anyone gotten back? Or, if you haven't sent an idea out, then you're constantly searching for something to *have* an idea about. You're looking for something new, somebody else's idea, some new report from the field, some new twist on an old story.

But the message I got a little after 8 that night fell into a different category. It was a message I'd been waiting for but never expected to get—not without many more pain-in-the-ass calls from me first.

It came from Robby Walsh's office, informing me that my interview request was being granted. Mr. Walsh would be available in the ayem tomorrow. He'd meet me at his house, just outside of Reno.

How about that: Just a few hours after a pair of jumpers try to fuck me over, Robby Walsh wants to talk.

I'm not drawing any conclusions— I'm just noting the proximity of time.


>>>


I caught a flight the next morning, rented a car and followed the directions they gave me. Interstate 80 east of Reno, then two turn-offs onto smaller roads. Dust blowing, clouds hurrying by, and that strange phenomenon of mountain country, where everything sounds like it's in the distance.

I was approaching the area where Robby's address was supposed to be when I saw a white granite mountain and some kind of high-altitude hallucination. The outlines of a house—a huge white glistening single-level house—seemed to be growing out of the base of the mountain. It was like the mountain was giving birth to the house.

No illusion. The exterior stone of Robby's residence was the same white granite as the mountain's and it was built right into the base. The house was an extension of the mountain, white granite molded out of white granite, the house melded into the mountain.

Impressive. Thing was, there was no way to get in. The house was semi-circled by a high white granite wall. There was no entryway, no opening. Where do you go from here?

I sat there, confused, until a guard appeared at the far end of the wall and waved me over. He was wearing a plain khaki uniform, a lapel-attached walkie-talkie and a large, prominently displayed holster on his right hip.

He anxiously studied my driver's license and *Real Story* ID. "You're expected." Sigh of relief all around.

He then told me where to drive and it seemed like he was saying to go straight *into* the mountain. Where? Then I saw it: A tunnel, a cave entrance, had been carved into the bottom of the mountain.

A second guard also made a nervous check of my creds at the entrance, then raised the barrier to let me through. Fluorescent high bays hung on the other side, lighting up a whole network of connecting passageways running beneath the mountain.

A third guard took my keys, wanded me with a hand-held scanner and asked me to hand over my Glock. Like the others, he was shaky but very polite and professional.

Yet another checked my name on his clipboard. "Mr. Walsh will see you in the drawing room," he said with a sense of announcement.

Among the many passageways available, he picked the one closest to us, taking me through maybe 150 underground feet of boulder-built white granite walls and supporting archways. The pace was slow, deliberate, almost hospital speed. We passed utility rooms— generators, water pumps. All the rooms were on one side of the passage, away from the body of the mountain.

A brass-grilled door took us into the house, into a wide sunlit hallway. We went past a library-study, a couple of guest bedrooms, all built again on the non-mountain side.

The guard dropped me off in the drawing room—which, really, was less suited for drawing than for constructing 600-seat Airbuses. A quick glance: thick roof beams of foxtail pine, a large white granite (of course) fireplace, a Steinway grand piano, various settings of couches and chairs decorated with geometric dream-catcher mandalas, artsy groupings of beaded Paiute baskets, a long red oak Mission table and chairs at one end, a pair of arches leading to the rest of the house. Probably take five minutes to walk to the end of the room and back.

Lobbyist—I've gotta get into this line of work.

There were two people in the room, standing by the Mission table. One was a grave, Armani-suited woman with a pair of rimless glasses, a green leather attaché case and a head of hair that looked like black cotton candy.

She introduced herself. "Esther Lazarev. Mr. Walsh's attorney."

The other was Mr. Walsh himself. Six-foot-four, conventionally handsome, big downshock of Bobby Kennedy hair covering his forehead, rocking on the balls of his feet like he was putting the universe on notice that he was standing in its center. His was wearing a white linen suit with a turquoise T-shirt. He'd watched too much Don Johnson growing up.

At least the T-shirt picked up his eyes, which were big and blue and filled

with some liquidy brightness. And with
nothing else. There was absolutely no
expression in his eyes, just this cool,
smooth vacuum of a look.

A perfect politician's face.

>>>

To give him equal time, here's Robby's
mini-bio:

•One thing you can say about him, he can
play basketball. He distinguishes himself
in school as a point guard with exceptional
ball-handling skills. Unfortunately, his list
of accomplishments ends there. A piss-
poor student of epic proportions, Robby
just manages to bumble through high
school, college and a third-rate law school.
He graduates with zero prospects. But he
does something smart.

•He marries Leah Hagler. Which is to say, he becomes Ken Hagler's son-in-law. Hagler, a state senator who was first elected around the time Moses was pulled out of the bulrushes, has become one of Nevada's most powerful pols. With Hagler's backing, Robby gets elected to the state legislature.

•Accusations of fraud are raised before, during and after the election. The charges run the gamut from vote buying and exploitation of voter confusion to ballot stuffing, missing ballots and intentional distribution of misinformation.

•Frequently absent, rarely casting a vote and demonstrating almost no understanding of issues, Robby is an inept in Carson City as he was in school. But he endears himself with one quality—he's a truly gifted fund-raiser. People might not respect his record but they sure do like him and they shell out the cash to prove it. Robby amply pads the war chests of fellow politicians, especially his own.

•On the strength of his campaign spending and Ken Hagler's influence, Robby is elected to Congress and then as governor of Nevada.

•Almost overnight, the level of bribery and kickbacks in Carson City increases threefold, according to law-enforcement sources. Questions come up about construction contracts and leasing deals. Blogs and op-ed pages go ballistic when Robby's wife, Leah, is appointed to a job in the Department of Natural Resources, even though she failed a state hiring exam.

•The State Attorney General launches an investigation into Robby's alleged corruption. Robby publicly defies the AG to prove a goddamn thing. His approval rating drops to 27%.

•By the time Robby is linked with Amanda Eston, the Justice Department has joined the party. They're looking into the charges of payoffs and shakedowns from a federal racketeering viewpoint. His alleged ties to organized crime are of particular interest. Rumors surface that the investigation is going wider than Robby's pay-for-play schemes. He could also be involved in conspiracies to commit murder.

•Robby is convicted on a variety of RICO charges, including conspiracy to commit

mail fraud and wire fraud and solicitations
of bribery. More rumors: Ken Hagler
engineered the conviction to punish Robby
for cheating on his daughter with Amanda
Eston. In any case, Robby does his three
years, then reinvents himself as a lobbyist.
He now represents land-development
firms, credit unions and gaming
organizations. He's still dependent, it's
said, on the good graces of his father-in-
law.

>>>

Yeah, Robby was one cool blank, and I
had no doubt he could maintain that
expression, or lack of one, for hours, days,
months, years. But about a minute into this
conversation, when he said he assumed I'd
talked to L.C. Martin and all I said was
yes, those empty eyes got filled fast and he

worked himself into full-fledged hissy fit. Fascination transformation: It started with his mouth, a pissy pursing of the lips, a muscular contraction that seemed to slowly stir the rest of his body, seemed to work it up and set his eyes on fire, until, moments later, he was snarling like a tiger with a dart in its ass.

"What *right*, what goddamn *right* does he have to fuck with my life?" Robby said. "What right does some washed-up actor have to keep fucking with my life all these years like this?"

His lawyer, Esther Lazarev, tugged nervously on her Armani sleeve. "Robby…"

"You know why he keeps doing this, you know why. Out of *jealousy*. Out of petty fucking *jealousy*."

Esther looked at me. "You said on the phone this was off-the-record?"

"I said it *could* be."

"It *is*."

"I don't *care*," said Robby. "He's been saying this shit about me for *years*, and for *years* nobody's believed him. And with good right. Cause these things, these things he says, they have no subtlety to them, they have no fucking *nuance*."

"Robby," said Esther, "let me talk."

He looked at her for a moment, then decided she wasn't there.

"For years, but I'm still here. I'm still kicking it. You see me? You see me standing here? I'm still *alive*. I'm still fucking *unobliterated*."

Esther released a profound but considered sigh.

Robby stopped, let his bile level out a bit.

"So you talked to him," he said to me. "He told you all about his *theories.*"

"I thought it was worth some inquiry."

"And do you understand them? Do you understand the, the fucking *mechanics* of them? The weird algebra of how all this could possibly have happened?"

"I'm not sure. Why I'm talking to you."

"Well I'll tell you. They make no sense because I'm innocent. Was innocent, am innocent, remain innocent. I remain *very, VERY* innocent!"

"Robby!" said Esther. "Will you *shut* up and let me talk?"

He stalked away from us, feelings hurt.

Esther faced me. "Let me tell you how I see conditions here. The accusations Mr. Martin has continuously made against my client have no basis in fact, and in point of fact border on the…"

I watched Robby while she talked, watched him wander over to a telescope that was tripoded in front of a window. He stared at a garden outside the glass— cactus, white granite boulders, sagebrush with white, yellow and pink flowers, tiny yellow and orange-tinged fiddleneck blooms, pink rose-like desert peach flowers.

"…he's kept himself aboveboard," Esther was saying, "and he's worked very hard at it all this time."

Robby swiveled around. "Some might dispute how hard I've worked, I know that. But I *have*. I've worked hard despite what happened to me, despite assholes like L.C. fucking Martin. I worked hard, and *this* is what I got for it." He stretched his arms to take in—I don't know—the room, the house, the nation. "This is what I *earned.*"

I settled for the house. "Some place you've got. What I like about it is that it's not ostentatious in any way, shape or form."

"And I'm not letting some has-been shithead actor take it away from me." He came back to the Mission table. "Some guy who, let's face it, is lost in some years-ago time warp, who in his eyes still thinks he's going for an Academy Award."

"Robby," said Esther.

"Of course, if you *believe* what he's saying—and maybe you do, how do I know—but if you happen to *believe* what he's saying about me, then at least accord me the respect of acknowledging that there's another point of fucking view here."

"I didn't say I believed him," I said. "I don't even know if he's believable."

Esther jumped all over that. "I'm glad you brought that up." She began pulling paperwork out of her green leather attaché. "We wanted to talk to you about believability. Believability specifically as regards to the video. If L.C. Martin is planning in any way to identify my client as the other participant in the video, we're going to dispute him. We're going to *fiercely* dispute him. Robby had nothing to do with the video."

Robby was staring at the papers on the table. He seemed to be pausing, trying to take a reading of some inner gauge. Then he turned and walked away again.

"How can people look at that thing," he muttered. "It's a horrible thing to watch."

Esther consulted her notes. "We've done our due diligence. We've gone over the entire one minute and 18 seconds of the video. We've examined it frame by frame."

Robby sauntered over to the grand piano. A vase of sagebrush flowers, yellow with pink centers, sat on the lid, along with a pair of shears. He picked up the shears and began trimming the stems of the flowers.

"Permit me to point a few things out to you," said Esther. "First, the lighting in the bedroom is quite poor. It's so dim that any conclusions drawn would immediately invoke reasonable doubt. In addition, the male's face is never seen. There's no full facial exposure, there aren't even flashes of his profile. And finally, his voice is never heard. Not a peep. No one can possibly identify the male as my client. It's not him."

"It's not me," Robby yelled from the piano.

"All this shows," I said, "is that identity is inconclusive. It doesn't mean it *isn't* him."

"That brings us to the question of distinguishing marks," said Esther. "I'm referring to the wine-colored pigmentation. The genital *birthmark*. You know what I'm talking about?"

"I've seen it."

"We're prepared to offer testimony that my client bears no such growth on any part of his body. We're prepared to offer sworn testimony from his wife and from himself. He has no such birthmark."

"Can you prove it hasn't been removed in the past five years?"

Esther got stung. "That's *offensive*. That's truly *disgusting*. I really think you've crossed a boundary."

"I'm just asking a question."

"Same fucking thing," yelled Robby. He put the shears down and came back to the table. "It's not me. I wasn't there. And if you publish *anything* that says to the contrary, you'll have the best and biggest fucking lawsuit in the recorded fucking history of the world on your head!"

"No need to shout."

"I'm making a *point*."

"It's a legitimate means of emphasis," said Esther.

"I'm not publishing anything at this point," I said. "I'm just trying to find the original video."

This ushered in a few seconds of silence. We suddenly seemed to have an awkward moment among us.

Esther began stuffing papers back in her case. "How's that going for you?"

"Not bad."

Robby shifted on his feet. "Do you know where it is?"

I looked at him. "Not yet, no."

"You can tell us," said Esther. "It's off-the-record."

"I'm still running it down."

I was lying, of course, and they both seemed to sense it.

Robby stood still. He looked like he was searching for something inside himself.

"I personally hope it never comes out," he said. "I think that would be best, you know, for everybody's sake."

"What do you mean by that?"

"I mean it's just a piece of voyeuristic trash. It's a dishonor to her memory. It disgraces who she was."

"Don't say anything else," said Esther.

"Let's go right at it," I said. "Were you involved with her?"

"Don't answer that!"

"Off-the-record."

"I think she was a wonderful actress," said Robby, "and a wonderful and generous person. That's my only comment."

"So maybe you were, maybe you weren't involved."

"I said what I said."

"How about Ken Hagler? Was he involved in anything about her?"

"*Robby.*"

Robby laughed. "My father-in-law? This has nothing to do with me and my father-in-law. This has nothing to do with me and Amanda. Has *everything* to do with me and your friend L.C. Martin."

"I don't think I'd call him a friend."

"Good. Cause me, I wouldn't wanna be anywhere around that fuck-faced amoeba right now. I mean what does he *feel* when he talks about me? Does he feel some kind of *glee* in it?"

"I have no idea what he feels."

"Well fuck him. I don't care. I really don't care. I mean if he was dying right in front of me, if he was choking on his own vomit, I wouldn't do a thing to help him."

"Robby, no more."

"No, check that. I *would* do something. I'd puke in his mouth and help him finish the task. I'd puke in his mouth and stand there laughing while he died."

The lobbyist, methinks, doth protest too much.

>>>

Driving back to Reno, I remembered a client we once had at the agency, back in my investigation days. She'd hired us to catch her husband cheating on her. Which we did. Many, many times. Finally she just gave up. *Women*, she said, *will be the death of him.*

Turns out she was right, but not in the way she intended.

One day, as he was crossing the street, he saw a gorgeous woman standing off to the right.

He never saw the car coming the other way until it hit him.

>>>

## HOW DO YOU DRESS
## FOR SUICIDE?

I needed a break. I needed a time-out from all this hollow-eyed, bone-scraping confrontation. Things were getting a little too *intense*. I called Tasha Eston. She'd said to let her know if I found anything out. We talked about Norridge Morris— yes, her sister's stalker was now the design muse behind Crazy Face. We talked about Robby Walsh, the dry-air insanity of that scene. She asked what I was doing now, did I have time to grab a bite? Great. Pick her up at her apartment and we'd get some dinner.

Tasha lived in West Hollywood, in a yellow-walled apartment that combined the living room and kitchen into one big space, with a landscaped balcony offering up a soul-singing view of the Hollywood Hills.

She was on her cell when she let me in. "You can't say it's made from *peat moss…*" she was saying. "Cause it associates with *bogs* and *swamps. Fertilizer. Compost…* No, say it's made from *sphagnum*—it's much better. Or just *moss…*"

One wall of the living room was stacked with samples of the organic products she repped. Shampoo, conditioner, styling creams, texturizing gels, moisturizers, cleansers, body treatments, lipstick, eye shadow, bronzers. A basket of folded laundry sat on the kitchen table. The apartment smelled like nutmeg and lemon, and so did she.

"I don't want to get caught on the sorry end of a trend, that's all…"

Another living room wall was cubed up with photos, mostly of Amanda. Studio portraits. Casual shots. Amanda riding a roller-coaster with Tasha, sparring with L.C., things like that. Then there were other photos, older ones. Adults in stiff poses, with empty, shadowed smiles. Family photos? A gallery of the dead?

Yes—when she got off the phone she pointed out who was who. Her mother. Her father. The uncle who'd shot himself with her father's .38. The cousin who'd killed her sleeping son and then herself. Aunt Renee with the son who'd jumped off the tallest building in Richmond. Grim etc., etc.

"The family thing," I said, "she couldn't escape it."

"No."

"But you could?"

"Took work."

That's how we end ended up at the kitchen table, laundry basket moved to the counter. Tasha made fresh ground, fresh brewed organic coffee.

It was the night for her, she said, always during the night. The nightmares started when she was a kid, got worse as she got older. Nightmares all night long— the faces of her mother, father and the others. The images of her father's blood-soaked sheet, the noose her mother had made out of a bedsheet.

"I don't think I ever really slept," she said. "Not until dawn, when I could get a couple of hours at most. But less and less of that as time went by. And the less sleep, the more I'd think about it during waking time. I'd think about killing myself all day long. Once I even tried to time the intervals—I was thinking about suicide every three or four minutes. They'd never go away. All I could hear in my head was death thoughts."

"And after a while they start sounding like they make sense."

"That's it. Very persuasive. Good sales techniques. That's when I realized, that point, I needed help. I wasn't going to make it unless I got help. I couldn't stop it by myself."

"What did you do?"

"Went to see a specialist, a psychiatrist who dealt with suicide attempts, suicidal ideation. She made me sign a No Suicide contract."

"That help?"

"It sounds ridiculous, but, yeah, it did. It's like a *promise*, you know? And she made me tell my story, my family's story. She made me tell it over and over and fucking over again. I thought that was ridiculous too, a billable waste of time, but gradually, the more I told it, the better I felt. The more I told it, I don't know, my mind just seemed to *adjust*."

"Sometimes that's all you need. A tiny adjustment. You change the way you look at things, just a bit, just an *inch*, and things that were terrifying are suddenly all right."

"An inch, right. Just an inch."

"Just an inch, and tragedy turns to comedy."

Tasha looked at me. "This happened to you?"

I laughed. "One of the times I tried to kill myself? Only thing that stopped me was I couldn't decide what to wear."

She kept looking. "It doesn't sound like you're getting this stuff from *Oprah*."

I turned and checked her balcony. Darkness was settling over the Hills.

I told her about my past—the booze, the meth, the manslaughter. I told her about getting into AA, getting into Buddhism in prison. I told her about dying to yourself to be reborn, how we're in the hands of something, how if you give yourself up enough to it you find out it's God, the moving mystery of God, always in motion.

"You go back," I said, "anthropology, you look at the old initiation rites? They all ended the same way. The ancient rites always ended the same way. With an acceptance of reality, an embrace of ordinary, everyday reality. That was the whole point of the rites, that was the big secret waiting to be discovered. The person getting initiated would always end up embracing the world just as it is."

She sipped her coffee, smiling. "You're kind of an interesting guy, you know that?"

"You know, I've always suspected something like that might be true."

>>>

We never made it to dinner, never made it out of the apartment. Instead we stayed in the kitchen and just kept talking about our lives, the things we'd learned, the things we were still trying to learn. But we *did* get hungry. Tasha had two-thirds of a blueberry pie in the fridge. Organic, of course. Sapphire Highbush berries from Fresno, grown in low, 4.8 pH soil, two-and-a-half feet between each plant. The pie was fantastic. Every bite sent my endorphins into a Niagra release.

The evening took a lazy drift into night. Who knew what time it was? I was feeling more relaxed than I'd been in a long, long time.

"I'm glad we know what we're saying to each other," Tasha said. "It's good to know, good to understand, right? Cause isn't that why we're saying these things to each other?"

The more she talked, the more attractive I found her. For me, nothing is sexier than character, and she had a lot of character.

I was telling her I needed to work on my patience, work on living one day at a time. Every morning I try to read a daily meditation? But I always keep skipping ahead, looking to see what the next days have to say.

She was rinsing the dishes in the sink, her back to me, while I was talking. Naturally I was staring at her ass. Incredible shape—completely organic, I'm sure. I don't know how it happened, but somehow she sensed where my eyes were.

She quickly turned around and gave me this I-know-what-you're-doing look. Busted. She didn't say anything, didn't do anything except turn back around and finish with the dishes.

She ripped off a paper towel—unbleached, undyed—dried her hands and walked over to the table. Not angry, not pleased, not nothing. I didn't know what she was going to do or say, and I was a little surprised when she asked did I want to go out on the balcony. The view, she said, was pretty nice.

It was. Moving into the living room area, you could see that the night sky was a dark purple, with a nearly perfect half-moon hanging high over the Hills. The view was so beautiful it could break your heart.

We never made it out to the balcony. As we walked toward the sliding door her leg brushed against mine. I took another step, trying to calculate if this was an accident. She brushed against my leg again. Uh-huh.

I took her hand, turned her toward me and pressed my mouth against hers. She smelled like nutmeg and lemon and night and wet earth. She hid her face under my jaw and nuzzled the flesh of my neck. I unbuttoned her top, slowly, no hurry, kissed her again, deeper this time, took off her top. It was all slow, very slow, taking relaxed time, undressing each other in suspended motion. I thought about Jimmy Reed singing *Caress Me*. That was the rhythm we were in, and the blues couldn't get any slower than that.

>>>

We never made it into the bedroom. I woke up on the area rug in the living room, about as rested as I've ever been. She was sitting up next to me, knees bent, gazing out past the balcony. The moon was getting ready to disappear behind the Hills now. You could almost see stars in the sky.

We both sat there for a minute, still naked, not saying anything, just letting the time zen by.

She shifted to me. "I was thinking of something. There's somebody maybe you should talk to."

Back down to earth.

"Who's that?"

"My sister's bodyguard."

"You know where he is?"

"She. And, yeah, we're still close. I know how to get her."

"Might help."

"She's never talked to anybody about that night. I mean, outside of the police, me, L.C. She's always refused to talk to anybody else, especially the media."

"She'll talk now?"

"I can call her, talk her around, tell her you're all right. Maybe she'll be around tomorrow."

"What's her name?"

"Pear Wicinski."

"What do you mean Pear? Like the fruit?"

"It was supposed to be Pearl, but they left the L off the birth certificate."

"Hell of a name to go through life with."

Tasha shrugged, I don't know. "She's done all right with it."


>>>

## THE FLYING WIG-RIPPER
## BODY SLAM

The building was an old, six-story tenement in Huntington Park, just off the Harbor Freeway, and with the weedy vegetation out front and the rope-bridges of drying wash strung from the upper windows, it still gave off a late 60's crash-pad vibe. I found a scotch-taped strip of paper handwritten *P. Wicinski*, pressed the button next to it and got buzzed in.

A9—the ground floor. A hallway lit with naked light bulbs, rusted sprinkler pipes crossing overhead, old wood redolent of aged urine and cheap cigars. Some cartoon soundtrack—it might've been *Chop Socky Chooks*—blared from one of the upper floors.

Pear Wicinski stood I'd say maybe only 5-3, but she had a big, broad face and even bigger, broader shoulders. Woman was built like a septuagenarian pork chop. She was wearing a faded, floral-print, smock-like housecoat and she walked with a cane.

"Quinn McShane?" I said. "*Real Story*?"

"Well whoopdee fucking doo."

"Tasha Eston called?"

"I know, I know. She spoke highly, as a matter of fact."

Pear let me in. I saw a ceiling fan circulating warm air through a cramped apartment, every square inch jammed with ancient furniture. A big red bottle of Kriss-Mist all-natural liquid laxative sat on the coffee table.

"Why is it," Pear wanted to know, "at my age, people still keep bothering me about this thing?"

Then I saw the walls. Her life story was on the walls. The spaces were all taken up by title belts, championship medals, certificates, photos of a much-younger Pear dressed in leopard-print leotards, sequined one-piece bathing suits, leather gowns, Carmen Miranda headdresses, framed newspaper clippings and wrestling magazine covers, posters billing her as The Wild Wicinski or The Wild Pear.

"You were a *wrestler*?"

"What makes you say that?"

Wiseass.

I moved closer to one of the newspaper stories, scanned the display type—the headlines and captions. "Says you were a leading figure on the women's circuit."

"No. I was *queen* of the women's circuit. Twelve-year period, except for a few months here and there, I held one version or another of every world championship title."

"Jesus that's some career."

She limped over to me. "My dad loved pro wrestling, started taking me to matches when I was, oh, 8, 9. One night I saw Baby Burgess, she was the reigning women's top dog at the time. She was short of stature, just like me, but she could bring it. That's when I got the calling, seeing Baby Burgess. I was an inch shorter than her, only weighed like 116 my first matches."

"And they said you wouldn't make it."

"But I had the moves. I had my specialties. The flying 180 drop-kick. The flying backward head scissors. The flying wig-ripper body slam. I made them my own. I'd get the house on its feet every time I did them."

She pointed her cane at a newspaper clipping showing her and another wrestler in a sequence of photos.

"This is the flying 180 drop-kick. You see? You've got your back to your opponent, looks like you're open for an attack. Then you make a flat-footed jump as high as you can, turn 180 degrees at the top of the jump and kick your opponent in the face or chest as the case may be. I could do a six-foot vertical from a flat-foot start."

"Looks like you had some fun."

"I wish I was still doing it. Age and injury said otherwise." She did a 180 and hobbled away from the walls. "Now look at this, 72 rat bastard years old and I'm gimping around like Walter Brennan in *The Real McCoys.*"

Her limp reminded me of Grady Alexander, dealing RD-17 or TT-44 or ABC-123 up in Topanga Canyon.

"Everybody's getting old," I said.

"I'm not getting old. I *got* old." Pear gestured to some indefinite part of the apartment. "I keep a folder with all my medical bills. Every year it keeps getting thicker and thicker."

I stepped next to her. "So after wrestling, a bodyguard?"

"Gradually. I stayed on the circuit for a while—trainer, manager, promoter. Then I got tired of all the sloppola. A few of the men fighters I knew, they'd gotten into security. Most of these guys, their heads were as empty as a coolie dental plan. I thought if they could do it, why not me?"

"For how long?"

"I was bodyguarding for a few years. Had some decent clients, some not so."

"Like?"

She shook her head. "Discretion. Say one thing, though. A lot of them? They were just camera trash, nothing more than that. Not Amanda, though. I was honestly fond of her. She was my last client, in fact. I retired after her, became a *pensioneer*."

"That's what I want to talk to you about. About Amanda."

"No shit," she sighed. "I know— Tasha said you were someone who could be trusted."

"I guess you've heard all the stories about her death."

"You mean have I talked to L.C.?" she laughed. "Yes, I've heard them all. He's bent my ear for many an hour, though I have to say I'm fond of him too. Him and Tasha both."

"What do you think about the stories?"

Pear sighed. "We're all different, no one's the same. We all have different dreams, different desires, different fabric softeners."

She picked something up from the coffee table, next to the Kriss-Mist—a small, delicate, lace handkerchief, which she pinned to her housecoat. An improbable accessory for her blue-collar body.

"We can talk," she said, "but not today. Some other time maybe."

"Mood's not right?"

"Not that a-tall. I'm on my way to the store. Got to get my shopping done."

"I'll drive you."

"I'm walking. I prefer to walk. I need the exercise."

"How about if I walk with you? I'd appreciate it."

She sighed again. "If you want to do some walking, I'll do some talking."

>>>

The streets were teeming, hundreds of people doing a heavy stroll under the hot sun. Angry traffic, horns and brakes snarling at each other. The smell of sweat mixed with street garbage. We took bulging, rippling sidewalks past liquor stores, bodegas, take-outs from every country in Asia, windows with herb-jars of borraja, gordolobo, tejocotes, ginseng and St. John's wort, hair-straightening places, signs for acupuncture and acupressure, nail salons, The ReSouled Shop—a

second-hand clothing store, bars, check-
cashing joints, AME storefront churches,
Pentacostal storefront churches. People
were sitting on stoops, crates or aluminum
chairs wherever shade was to be found.
Dope-sick stoners slumped against the
walls.

Pear, with her cane and lace
handkerchief, was promenading along like
we were walking down Rodeo Drive.

"I took it in my face," she was
saying. "Really, that's where I felt it. The
moment I walked into that room, found
her lying there, I remember my cheeks
turning solid and heavy. I could feel all the
weight of my years in my face."

"You saw her when last?"

"That afternoon. She had a meeting
in Century City, talking about *Purple
Blues*. I took her over there, brought her

home, went inside for a few minutes, we talked, I left."

"You called that night, but no answer."

"That's when I rushed over."

"Why did you call?"

"I called every night, at least once. That was the ritual we had. She was a bad sleeper, always waking up. And every time she woke up—this was sometimes seven, eight times a night—she'd check the alarm and the locks. She had a mania about it. Every time she got up, she'd check the doors, the windows, the security. I'd call to make sure everything was all right."

"Even if she had company?"

"*Every* night. She wanted me to call at least once a night. Most times she'd say everything was fine, but check back in an hour or two."

"So when you called that night, you knew something was wrong."

Pear nodded. "No answer, I knew. Rushed over right away. The doors were all locked, the windows. The alarm was still on. If anybody else had been there that night, she let them in."

"You know what L.C. thinks, right? Somebody had keys made, knew the codes?"

"There we disagree. One of the many things L.C. and I disagree on. She was too light a sleeper. Anybody trying to get in, *any* sound, she would've purely panicked. She would've woken bolt up and called me or 911."

"And she didn't."

"No call made, no locks opened, no alarm turned off. If anybody *was* in there, it was someone she knew."

A homeless woman stumbled up to us. She had skin the texture of Astroturf and was wearing a Hillcrest Country Club T-shirt. "The Lord be with you don't touch me," she said.

Pear never broke stride and limped right past her. I followed. The woman muttered something and walked away.

"You ever meet Robby Walsh?" I said.

"Plenty of times. He was over there three, four times a week. Must've *always* had a boner on. Or, as the French say, a *bonair*."

"You think she could've heard him talking about things, the pressures he was under?"

She laughed. "We're back to L.C. now? All his jabber-wabber? I'll tell you something, my opinion, if Robby had anything to do with her dying, nobody will ever prove it."

"Why not?"

"You ever know a Peeping Tom who kept *his* blinds open?" She knocked a stone out of the way with her cane. "I'll say one thing about Robby, though. She seemed pretty happy when he was around. I don't know for sure, we didn't discuss her specific intake, but I don't think she was as stoned when he was around. She just seemed a lot less irritable and argumentative."

"No fighting?"

"No fighting?" Pear stopped, looked at the cracked sidewalk. "The afternoon I dropped her off, the last time? We were talking, she got a call. Took it in the bedroom, but I could hear her hotting it up with somebody. Saying, I'm tired of this, no more of this shit, I've had it."

"You don't know who?"

She shook her head and began walking again. "And she didn't say anything about it when she came out. Wasn't my place to ask."

We were coming up on our destination, Schirmer's Market. A guy in a dashiki was hawking incense off a card table on the edge of the tiny parking lot. Three of the neighborhood pervs, somberly watching the street, sat on an aluminum-colored couch that had been propped up against the market wall.

"Have you seen the video?"

"I have to say I have," she said. "I didn't like doing it, not at all, but it felt like I *had* to. I was looking for a clue or something, trying to understand what happened."

"Was she in the habit of making videos like that?"

"I wouldn't know. I know she enjoyed the bedroom, that much I know. But what she did in there I couldn't say. Not my purview."

The three pervs weren't lounging on the aluminum couch any more. They were suddenly in front of us, standing straight in our faces.

One of them, a guy with a cigarette in his mouth and a greasy ponytail tied up in a bun at the back of his head, stepped up to me. He was a rapid smoker, puffing every three seconds like a steam locomotive.

"The fuck you think you are?" he said to me.

"Sorry?"

"You won't talk. You won't help out. You won't cooperate. The fuck? What's wrong with you?"

"T's right, man," the second guy behind him said. "The fuck?" This was a big, barrel-chested dude with the belly of a pregnant woman. He was quite a sight.

The third one, a long-haired tweaker, actually wasn't a bad looking guy, nothing a full set of teeth couldn't fix. He didn't say anything. The silent but violent type.

I looked at Rapid Smoker. "What do you want?"

"You hear that? What do we want." He worked that cigarette like a smoker at the airport getting ready to take a long flight. "You're pissing people off. You're making them angry. You're making them *bitter*."

I saw the guy selling incense step back from his card table and look away. He didn't want to be part of this.

"*Bitter*?"

"You don't know how bitter."

I was sweating mud. They pull this shit with a cripple old lady right here? Any other time I would've put my hand on the Glock under my hoodie, but I wasn't going to pull it out, not with Pear around.

Who now leaned forward on her cane. "It's nice they let you boys go out and play by yourselves," she said, "but shouldn't you have *some* supervision?"

Rapid Smoker ignored her. "You sure you know what you're doing?" he said to me. "Cause if you think I give a shit bout who you think you are, that's just sad. Tell you right now, that's just fucking sad."

He flicked the butt away and reached under his shirt. I saw the glint of something stuck in his belt, jumped away as he yanked the gun out. I saw him raise his arm, level the piece at me, then saw something come swooping through my line of vision, arching out of the sky.

Pear's cane came down hard on his wrist, knocking the gun to the ground. He grabbed his paining hand, turned his eyes to her and was about to turn his body and go after her when she whacked the cane across his lower spine. He fell screaming to the pavement, clutching at his back.

"Just a little bruise of the vertebra," she said. "Stop whining."

The big guy, Pregnant Belly, lunged at me, hands going for my shoulders. I uppercut his open mouth. The shot produced a moment of numbness in his eyes and not much else. His grappling-hook hands kept reaching for me. I threw punches between his arms, pounding his thick chest with all the effect of beating on a mountain.

I felt him grab my hoodie, start
swinging me, hurling me to the side, doing
a 180 on me, a 360, a 540, a 620. Finally
he let me go. I landed splat-flat against the
side of a Nissan Versa. I saw the third guy,
Silent But Violent, moving in on Pear, but
she was holding him off with the cane,
feinting at him, jabbing, swiping at his
head.

Pregant Belly charged at me again,
arms stretched out for another centrifugal
toss-around. I'm thinking, stay away from
the upper body. Tackle low. I pushed off
from the Versa as he came in, dove under
his arms and gave him a running head butt
in his soft round belly. He *oofed* and
staggered six or seven feet and probably
would've regained his balance, but he'd
stumbled just far enough back to collide
with the incense-laden card table. The
dashiki guy jumped into the clear as

Pregnant Belly wrestled with the table, carrying it back another four or five feet and scattering Sandalwood, Egyptian Musk and Raspberry Fantasy joss sticks all over the ground until the table gave way and tumbled over and he went down with it.

I looked over at Pear, looked just in time to see Silent But Violent kicking the cane out of her hands. I started running as the guy was reaching back to throw a punch at her head. No need. As his arm was moving Pear grabbed his long hair, twisted around and threw him and his momentum over her shoulder, smacking him to the ground with thudding, pancaking force.

I think I've just witnessed a demonstration of the flying wig-ripper body slam.

"You all right?"

"My back is killing me," said Pear. "But a hot bath I'll be okay. Hand me my cane."

I once interviewed a 90-year-old woman who'd been an outstanding tap dancer in her prime. She could barely walk when I met her, but she could still do a triple time step.

I saw the incense guy pick up Rapid Smoker's gun and slip it under his dashiki. Fair exchange, I guess, for his damaged merchandise.

One by one, our three friends wobbled to their feet. Pregnant Belly and Silent But Violent didn't hesitate—they started scrambling away. Rapid Smoker made a quick look for his piece and, not finding it, went to join them. But first he glanced at me.

"God do people hate you," he yelled, and took off.

"What's the what on all that?" said Pear.

"Something to do with the video."

"*Those* turds?"

"Sent by somebody."

"Who?"

"Somebody with money. Somebody with power. I have my suspicions."

She turned and started heading for the entrance of Schirmer's Market. "Well, at least I got my exercise in."

"You shouldn't have done that. Too dangerous."

"What difference does it make?" she shrugged. "At my age, it's too late to die young."

>>>

# >>>CHAPTER 5

## >>THE CORE
## OF THE MAZE

**WHERE GOD HIDES**

The house was a single-level Traditional in Brentwood, located just a few manicured blocks away, ironically, from where O.J. Simpson used to live. The exterior walls were made of diagonal mahogany slatting, with columns of French limestone at the corners. The sloped roof meant there were vaulted beam ceilings inside. This is where Amanda Eston lived, and where she died.

Tasha and I sat in her car, staring at the house across its deep set-back. She was pointing out what had changed in five years. The eucalyptus trees were new. So were the shrubs, though they needed a trim. The pool and enclosed lanai were the same. The blinding white gazebo in the back, trust her, was a new addition.

Her eyes kept returning to the house. "So much went on in there. Good, bad. She spent so much time trying to level her life out. Sometimes I think…" Tasha turned away and looked at the street. "Sometimes I'm almost sorry I found out what I did, about the family, the history. Maybe it was too much for her, too much burden. Maybe things would've been different, maybe her brain circuitry would've been different, if she didn't know. If I didn't know. If I hadn't gone back and looked."

"You *had* to go back," I said, "especially when you're young. No kid can resist something that's hidden. You can't keep children from trying to learn secrets, even when the child is yourself."

"I guess."

"Shit, that's the whole key to childhood. Trying to decode the secrets of life."

She glanced up through the trees. Endless blue, hot butter sun. The sky was looking very Mexican today.

"Pear's really all right?" she said.

"She's fine. Little backache is all."

"Maybe I shouldn't have gotten you together. I didn't know I'd be putting her in danger."

"She can take care of herself."

"Sometimes you take a bad path, you get lucky, you're still waiting for yourself on the other side."

I didn't get it. Then I realized she wasn't talking about Pear anymore.

"But how many times can you get away with it?" she went on. "Cause you know that one day you'll take that path and you *won't* be there on the side. But you still do it. You still try to run past the past, get way beyond it. Sometimes I... I used to wake up with the dead in my room. I could feel them there. My mother, my father, all of them. In my bedroom, waiting for me to join them."

I looked over at her. The tears were already running down her face.

I took her hand. Her fingers were coiled and shaking.

"It's all right," I said. "You'll be all right. You took the path, you found yourself on the other side. You'll *always* find yourself on the other side. Have some faith in that."

She looked again at the house, the property. "You see the back, how leafy it is?"

Beyond the gazebo the yard was thick and hidden with magnolia trees and high bushes.

"There was a spot like that where we lived," Tasha said, "just down the street from our house. All woodsy and shady. My mother always said that's where God hides. He hides in the woods so no one can find him."

She took her hand away from mine, wiped her cheeks and eyes. Seconds of silence went by.

"Do you believe in an afterlife?" she said.

"I don't know. I'm just trying to deal with *this* life."

She nodded and said my name. Quinn. Then she said it three or four times and leaned across the seat to me. Leaned so close I could smell the light sweat of her body. We kissed. We held each other

and kissed again, all the bio-chemistry
instantly up and running. We were making
out in her car, making out in front of the
house where her sister's body had been
found.

>>>

## LET'S MAKE A DEAL

They were busy at the bureau chasing down a story on the actor Evan Striker. The guy's DUI hearing had been scheduled for today, and he didn't help his case by showing up drunk. The courtroom was chaos. Striker got angry because the judge got angry. "But I didn't *drive* here!" he protested.

I was busy with a call that came in.

*My name's Marvin Brackett. I know someone… I represent someone…who would like to do, like to do some business with you.*

His voice, though halting, was polished and practiced.

"What kind of business would that be?"

*If I tell you… If I say I'd rather not talk about it on the phone, will you, will you understand?*

"I'm not sure."

*It concerns something, something that's taken up a lot of your time lately. I believe... I believe it's taken up a great deal of your time...in the last, in the last few days. Am I making myself clear?*

What else *could* it be?

"I think so."

*The person, the person I represent, he's just trying to...trying to, you know...trying to...*

"Make some kind of deal?"

*Well what else would you expect? Yes, make, make a deal. Are you willing to meet?*

"Yes."

*How about tonight? We'll need some, need some privacy. Is 1 a.m. too late for you?*

Marvin Brackett gave me instructions and directions. My brain was on full hum when I hung up. Some odd little stew was cooking up. Somebody somewhere was crock-potting something.

## ADD TURPENTINE TO YOUR LIFE

I woke fast and had no idea where I was. My apartment? The Four Seasons? Tasha's bedroom—she was still sleeping next to me. I got the geranium smell of her skin, the fresh jasmine of her perfume. Her bed faced her balcony and the view beyond. The moon was blurred by mist on the Hills. They made me think, for a moment, of the Blue Ridge Mountains.

Her eyes were opening. She sat up, all smiles and wonder. We talked for a few minutes, nothing gigantic, just lazy talk, the little things you say after coming out of that secret sleep.

But Amanda wasn't far off from the center of her mind. Amanda and her family legacy. She brought the conversation back to her doubts.

"You never can tell," Tasha said. "You never know what's going on underneath. Maybe I should've never come to LA. Maybe I should've stayed in Virginia, never talked to her."

"I don't know. No matter what you do, where you go, you always end up facing yourself. Her, you, me—we all have to deal with ourselves."

We talked about escaping, or thinking you're escaping. I told her about my meth runs, staying up for days on crystal and booze, how reality gets so spread out it's as thin as a sheet of black ice. It's like adding turpentine to your life—the colors eventually get so diluted that everything ends up looking washed-out and fake.

She was gazing past her balcony. "Drugs," she said. "How much do you know about pralicin?"

"Very little."

"That's one thing that still bothers me. I know she did it herself, killed herself, but where did she get all that pralicin?"

"Was she doing it before?"

"Never—not as far as I know. I mean that's the thing. Hardly anybody ever did pralicin. It wasn't something you could just cop off the street. So where did she get it?"

I didn't say anything, but I was thinking: Maybe she went to a specialist dealer. Maybe she went to somebody who dealt unique kinds of drugs. Who did I know like that?

>>>

## AN ALTERNATIVE SCENARIO

Dodger Stadium was empty, but North
Hill Street nearby was jumping. People
strolling along eating *banh mi* subway
sandwiches, clothes shoppers trolling the
curbside bazaars for 1 a.m. bargains. I was
looking for a restaurant called The Fruit of
the Mekong, but Marvin Brackett told me
I'd never find it by name. He'd said not
only was the place's name written in
Vietnamese, in *quoc ngu*, but it was
spelled out in old Chinese sinograph
characters. Instead I should look for three
yellow apricot flowers painted on the
white awning outside.

Got it, just up ahead. Three flowers
side by side in slot-machine perfection.
The restaurant looked dark and crowded at
the same time. I kept walking, casually
moving another 100 feet or so past it,
glancing around at the night life. But

really searching for anything unusual. For anybody in the crowd who might be looking at *me*.

Nothing. I went back and into the Fruit of the Mekong. The hostess by the door was wearing a purple *ao dai*—a long, tight-fitting silk skirt—over the traditional pair of pants.

"Reservations?" she said.

"Not here to eat. I'd like to see someone about catering."

"Catering, yes." She took her eyes away from me. "I can help. When is your event planned for?"

"Thirteen days from now."

"I see. And how many people are you expecting?"

"Thirty-seven and a half."

The hostess nodded three times. "This way."

She brought me closer to the mobbed bar area, where the laughter seemed to notch up an octave into a giggle as we approached. Two women were standing at this end of the bar, staring at each other, one running her hand through the other's hair.

The hostess guided me to a pair of red velvet drapes hanging near the side of the bar. "Up the stairs, two doors to the right."

I passed through. Old staircase, sagging steps, barely lit. Very quiet. I kept my hand on the Glock.

The second door to the right opened to a small private dining room— one table, three chairs. Two people were seated.

One was a stunning woman with long black Hispanic hair, dark skin against a business suit the color of a pink Cadillac.

She said her name was Paloma Applewhite, her voice as musical and passionate as Yolanda Vega calling out the lottery numbers in New York—and tonight's *bonus* number is *fawty-four*!

The other was a squat, powerfully built man with a well-cut suit, a squash-shaped head and a military buzzcut.

"Marvin Brackett. We talked, we talked on the phone."

"I thought your voice was familiar."

Poloma beamed. "Have a seat, *please*!"

They were drinking coffee, a pot with extra cups and saucers on the table. She asked if I wanted some and poured. Three people sitting around drinking coffee at one in the morning. It was like a mini AA meeting.

"*Thank* you for coming," said Paloma. "I guess you're wondering what you're doing here."

"The thought occurred to me."

"Sorry for all the, all the mystery," said Marvin.

"We'll try to answer *all* your questions."

She handed me a business card. *Elegant Acquisitions. Paloma Applewhite, President.*

"We're speaking to you," she said, "on behalf of a certain party, a certain *individual.* He's a collector, an *avid* collector."

"He's very, he's very enthusiastic about his interests."

"Yes, and he's taken an *extreme* interest—let me emphasize, an *EXTREME* interest—in Amanda Eston."

I got it now. Palomoa was an LA equivalent of Arnoud Shuyler.

"There's a certain *artifact* on the market right now, a certain Amanda Eston collectible, that he has a *keen* desire to buy. We have reason to believe you're *also* trying to buy it."

"Am I?"

"We're talking, *obviously*, about the video."

"The full, the full version of the video. The original.

I sipped my coffee. "What do you know about the video?"

"Everybody knows *something* about the video. It's a very *popular* topic."

"And what can I do for you?"

Poloma settled into her pitch. "We assume you're acting on behalf of *Real Story*. You're conducting all these *arduous* negotiations in their name. We *assume* your organization sees it as a valuable piece of property."

"Assume away."

"Let's say you succeed. Let's say you *finally* manage to make the purchase for *Real Story*. What do you get out of it?"

"Get out of it?" I shrugged. "Satisfaction of a job well done."

She and Marvin smiled at each other.

"Is that *fair*? Do you think it is? With all the work you've done, with *everything* you've gone through, is it fair that you received no objective compensation?"

More coffee for me. "Your question doesn't answer the question. What am I doing here?"

Poloma looked at Marvin and angled her head a bit to the right. Marvin nodded.

"Let me propose an *alternative* scenario. Let's say the attempt to acquire the video becomes too *complicated*, too *tricky*, and *Real Story* decides it's not worth it. Let's say you *tell* them that. The difficulties have queered you off the deal. Things have become too volatile, too *hairy*."

Too hairy. As in people trying to jump me almost everywhere I go?

"They'd take your word for it, *wouldn't* they? They'd withdraw their bid."

"They might."

"Let's say it happens. Let's say they drop their interest, only you keep negotiating. But now you're negotiating on *our* behalf. On our *client's* behalf. And let's say the deal *does* get made. We'll pay you a commission, a finder's fee. Our client will pay you 10 percent of the final sale price."

"What do you… What do you say to that?"

"I'd say it's backstabbing. Betrayal."

"I'd say it's *preserving* one's own self-interest. You're doing the *same* thing you're doing, but you're doing it for your own benefit."

"You know, there's a big difference between the words *contraceptive* and *scumbag*. They refer to the same object, but they don't mean the same thing."

Paloma gave me a full bright-white smile. "You know what you need to do? You need to dream more *elaborate* dreams. That's what you need to do. Let's say, round numbers, the video goes for 10 million. That's a million dollars in your pocket. Cash. Tax-free. Isn't that more *equitable* compensation?"

"You can, you can do something where we all make out. If you just, you know… If you just… You know?"

"Absolutely. Marvin's *absolutely* right."

I finished my coffee. "Then what's the next step?"

Paloma: pure joy.

"That's a *very* sensible question. I *applaud* you for it. Next step, I believe, is meeting with our client, coming to terms. Whatever *Real Story*'s offering, he'll top it. Are you agreeable to that?"

"When?"

"We'll call you, we'll *let* you know the arrangements."

"All the information, all the information you'll need, will be…will be relayed."

"We'll be in touch. Any questions? Any problems? *Good*. I think I can say that in just a *very* short time, we'll all be wearing our happy, *happy* shirts."

>>>

Well this was a new approach, a whole new twist in the stream. The let's-work-together approach. I liked it. I had a feeling I was finally getting to the heart of this crazy crapshoot.

The streets were still crowded, people bargain-hunting, wandering into the barbecue delis for roast goat or suckling pig. The night sky was purple from the street lights.

I felt like sonar was bouncing off the moon and into my brain.

As Paloma would say, let's say this is all part of the same plan, all part of the same too-*hairy* gambit. Let's say all those run-ins—at Schirmer's Market, in the parking garage, in Santa Monica, maybe even in Amsterdam—let's say there were all designed to make me take this deal. They were all designed to drive me into the safe and profitable arms of Paloma Applewhite and Marvin Brackett.

I'm thinking, if I go along with it, they'll lead me directly to the core of the maze. They'll lead me directly to—well, who?

Robby Walsh?

His father-in-law, Ken Hagler?

Or whoever who?


>>>

## RIGHT OUT FRONT

It didn't take me any 40 minutes to find the place this time. Dirt roads, mountains, woods thick enough to make you believe gods were living there. The sun wasn't as bright today, though. It kept fading in and out, shifting the shafts of light between the trees with laps of yellow and gray.

As I drove, I noticed my hands kept sticking to the wheel.

Here we go—the low-walled, thatched-roof, pine-paneled house, a Shinto temple lost in the forest. Grady Alexander answered the door in another one of those Yukata-style kimonos. He raised a finger, pressed it from his moustache to his goatee. Quiet. He had company.

I followed his lopsided, one-leg-longer stride inside. A girl with long, straight, iron-flat blond hair sat on a bench in front of the 54-inch screen. No squishy, soothing lava-lamp images on the big monitor this time. Instead, Wile E. Coyote was consulting a book titled *The Art of Road-Runner Trapping*, the cartoon's volume turned down to a whisper.

The girl looked scared. She had her arms wrapped around themselves, rocking backwards and forwards on the bench like a Jew davening to her prayers. She might've been 18, but I doubt it.

"She's having a tough trip," Grady low-spoke. "She dropped some AC-8, should be a soft high, more on the abstract side. Really a lovely buzz. But she started getting woozy, hyper, bad things running through her head, ruining through her head."

"Glockenspiel," the girl said. "All the otherworlders, they all know how to play the glockenspiel."

Grady leaned close to her. "Remember, everything's connected by rhythm, by the beat. The whole universe. You find the right rhythm, you ride with it, surf it out. You'll be all right."

He pulled me away and took me across the room. We stood by the ladder leading up to his bird's nest balcony-bedroom. How was I doing? Getting closer to cleaning up the mess? Much closer— very close. He was glad to hear it.

"I have a question for you," I said. "I'm gonna ask it right out front. You ever handle pralicin?"

"Pralicin? No. Why?"

"That's what killed Amanda Eston. An overdoes of pralicin."

"I don't flip that shit. It's like a narcotic, it's just a *numb-er*. It's just a body drug—there's no head to it."

"You never dealt it."

"Nah."

"Never."

"What'd I say?"

"Not even like five years ago?"

Grady went bewildered. "Wait. *Wait*. What're you asking?"

"I'm asking."

"You think it was *me*? You think I had something to *do* with it?"

"I might be getting a little paranoid," I conceded.

"*Might* be?"

His ringtone went off. Coiling Middle Eastern guitar. Tinariwen, wailing from the Libyan desert.

He hobble-stepped away to take the call.

"...yeah, uh-huh, just got a fresh batch in... Same price... No, no, you have something to do, don't take it all at once... No, from the Indian guy, Durjaya. You know him… Right, brilliant guy, lots of talent… No, that's not a third eye. That's a *birthmark*."

Grady returned the cell to his kimono and came back to the ladder. "What the hell're you talking about with the pralicin?"

"Sorry, just trying to get some answers."

"Is it a good sign when a drug dealer has to tell you you're paranoid?"

"Let me rephrase the question. If she killed herself, where would she get enough pralicin for a lethal dose?"

Grady stared at the sun spread across the floor, streaks turning overcast and then bright again. "Maybe she didn't have to."

"What do you mean?"

He took a seat on one of his short Japanese wooden benches. I sat on one opposite him.

"I told you the first time, I don't know much about Amanda Eston. I don't follow that world. But she had drug problems, right? Drugs and drinking?"

"She did."

"Was she taking any anti-addiction meds? Did she have scrips for any of those ween-off drugs?"

"I don't know."

"Cause if she'd gotten drugs like that from her doctor, or even if she had certain kinds of street drugs in her system, it could make all the difference."

"Make what difference?"

"One thing I know about pralicin, it's a strong inter-actor. A strong inter-actor and a strong metabolizer. If she'd taken any of those dependence-blockers during the day, then taken pralicin on top of that, she could've created a pharmacological nightmare."

"Accidentally killed herself?"

"Totally. And it wouldn't take much. Just a little pralicin can produce some nasty interactions with other drugs, especially the addiction drugs. The combination could've metabolized to some severely toxic levels. On an autopsy, it might even show up as a ridiculously high amount of pralicin."

"Even though she only took a little."

"What I'm saying. Could've been sheer accident. So all this, this what, *controversy* over her death? It could mean nothing. Her death was accidental."

"There is no death."

It was the girl. She was standing next to us now, a dreamy, whacked-out, wonder-struck look on her face.

"People don't die," she said. "Their energy just changes form. Nobody dies. The energy changes and goes back to its source, then comes back as a different vibration."

"Feeling a little better?" said Grady.

"It's all water," she said. "All of us are water. We're water before we're born. We're water after we die."

Wisdom from the mouths of stoned teen babes.

>>>

## THE BACK WAY

As promised, Marvin Brackett called: *The client, the client wants to meet tonight. Is that do, is that doable by you?*

"It's fine. Whereabouts?"

*Go to 919... 919 Sunnyland Street. Just off East...Olympic Boulevard.*

"Just off East Olympic Boulevard."

*Right. You know where it is?*

"I know the area."

*Just south of the 101...Santa Ana Freeway.*

"Okay."

*Just east, just east of the railroad tracks.*

"What time?"

*The client suggests 11:40. Tonight.*

"Kind of early for you, isn't it?"

Marvin didn't get my little joke.

*Can you be there?*

"Yes."

*Come in, come in through the back way.*

>>>

Tasha didn't know how to take the accidental-overdose theory. Surprise, sadness, skepticism. Three parts equal. She sat at the kitchen table, trying the explanation out in her mind, always coming up confused. If it's true, where does that leave everything?

Sometimes," she said, "I feel like I'm watching my life through a window."

But she *did* know how to take the news about the 11:40 meeting. She didn't like it.

"That's not a great neighborhood at night. Very isolated. Why does it have to be there?"

"I don't know. Guess there's only one way to find out."

"There's no way it sounds good."

"Who knows. It might even be fun."

"*Fun?*"

"If I live through it, I'll give you a definitive word."


>>>

## A MIRROR OVER MY HEART

Twenty minutes to midnight the air was sweating with heat. A cyclone fence surrounded 919 Sunnyland Street—just a warehouse in a row of many others. The fence's gate had been left open, although there were no cars or trucks in the parking lot. Neither in the front nor, as I drove around the building, in the back. Just an uninviting series of loading bay doors.

I pulled in front of the third door. A waxing half moon hung in the sky above. It looked like it had been plastered up there by the City of Los Angeles.

Per Marvin's instructions, I honked three long times, followed by two shorter blasts. Eight seconds later the bay door rose up like a curtain on a stage.

Only one area inside the warehouse was lit by overhead lamps. The dark rest of it was crammed with steel shipping containers and stackable crates, lit only by small, wire-meshed bulbs running along the walls. No sounds except for the whirring drones of electrical generators.

The lone lit area showed two cars already parked, a few crates scattered around, a concrete floor rich with trash—poles, steel cable, rectangles of cardboard. A battered old metal desk had been dragged into the middle of the space. Had to be for this meeting—there was no other reason for it to be where it was.

Four people were waiting. Marvin Brackett was standing by the desk, wearing the same suit from last night. Paloma Applewhite was next to him, smiling against a beige suit.

Sitting at the desk was a man who strongly resembled a big fat contented baby, one who was used to getting his milk supply whenever he wanted. He wore a brown linen suit, a checked dress shirt and a bowtie, plus a pocket handkerchief AND a carnation in his lapel. Old World overdose.

His name, I learned after I parked my car next to the others, was Hugo Brock. Yes, he was the collector.

Hunched at the desk on a small chair next to him was a guy with scarred knuckles, a leather jacket and a very attractive boil on his face. Quinton Foster, introduced as Mr. B's assistant, though he looked a lot more like a bodyguard.

Quinton was eating cherries out of a ripped plastic bag on the desk, spitting the pits and stems on the floor. He ate in a manic hurry, like finishing the bag was something he had to accomplish before he died.

Strange scene, these four people dwarfed by the cavernous space around them. There was something about the weirdness of it that was almost holy.

Hugo Brock spoke in a smooth, velvety calm voice. He sincerely hoped, he said, that we could engage in a fruitful conversation.

"I sit before you, Mr. McShane, with a mirror over my heart."

"Excuse me?"

"Eight hundred years ago, Genghis Kahn outfitted his warriors with mirrors over their hearts. It was an essential part of their armor. The Mongols were convinced that a heart-mirror was capable of turning away enemy powers, even enemy weapons. Or so Marco Polo tells us. In any case, I sit before you with my own mirror over my heart. My mirror is my love for Amanda Eston. My mirror, my protection, is my deep and abiding love for Amanda Eston."

"He's the perfect, the perfect buyer," said Marvin

"I have a *wonderful* feeling about this," said Paloma. "Nothing is going to *schmutz* it up."

Quinton kept working his way through the cherries.

I leaned against one of the crates. "So you're a big fan."

"Fan," said Hugo, "would be putting it mildly."

"What was her first professional job?"

Hugo laughed. "You're giving me a *test*?"

Marvin and Paloma weren't wearing their happy, happy shirts.

"That's not really, really necessary."

"You're kind of walking the *line* here."

"It's fine," said Hugo. "She performed her first professional job when she was quite young. It was a commercial, a television spot for St. Joseph's Aspirin. She played a child with a terrible fever."

"She had a tattoo of a mermaid. It was on her right shoulder."

"Of course."

"It had to be digitally removed for a movie. Which one?"

"*I'm Still Waiting*. A very successful comedy, a very liberal interpretation of Sandra Dee's *If A Man Answers*. Though I don't think Sandra Dee had to do any nude scenes."

"What was the name of Amanda's aunt?"

"Her aunt." Hugo curled forward on the desk, giving it some thought. "She was very close with her aunt. The woman raised her after her mother was sent away."

"That's right. And?"

He half closed his eyes. "Very close. They were very close."

Quinton was staring at me, though he never stopped popping those cherries.

Hugo's lips were moving, like he was saying a silent prayer. "*Renee*. Aunt Renee. She's buried here. The family couldn't afford a decent funeral. Amanda had her Aunt Renee buried here."

"Very good. You know your Estonology."

"I know my dreams, Mr. McShane. I know what I'm dreaming, and I know I have the energy to make it real. My energy is quite large. Let's talk money."

"Why not?"

"Where does it stand right now? How much is *Real Story* bidding?"

"Twenty million."

Just a *tiny* exaggeration.

"Twenty." Hugo turned his head to the open bay door, looked out at the industrial night. "All of us, I'm sure, are uncomfortable with beggars. I'll go to 25. Is that agreeable?"

"That's 2.5 *million* to you," said Paloma.

"Sounds good."

"Excellent. Finer words can't be said." Hugo nodded to Paloma and Marvin. "Now let's work out some details. Let's settle what we can at this point."

He glanced again at the open bay. "That door is making me nervous. Quinton, would you close it, please? Let's have some semblance of privacy."

With a superbly sullen attitude, Quinton spit a pit, got up from behind the desk and went for the door. I watched him as he walked, though not out of any intrinsic interest in him. Just curious. Why close the door now?

That's when I saw the black gleam at his feet. He was wearing a pair of black patent leather lace-up boots. I'd seen them before, in the parking lot in Santa Monica, at the mythical 317 Emory Road. When I was hiding under a Suburu Forester and taking a worm's-eye view. And he was wearing a multicolored ski mask.

How many pairs of those boots can there be?

That's how I knew. This was a set-up. This was no negotiation. It was an ambush, a trap.

Quinton took hold of the pendant switchbox hanging by the door and pushed a button. The bay slowly began to close.

Hugo was saying something about unregulated cash transfers.

"I have one more question," I said.

"Of course."

"Do you know who you are?"

Silence. Just the door settling down, the electrical generators humming away.

Hugo didn't know whether to smile or not. "Pardon?"

"Do you know who you are?"

"Are you serious?"

"What're you, what're you talking about?" said Marvin, he and Paloma both during a nervous shuffle.

"I'm serious. Do you know who you are?"

"Of *course* I know who I am."

"How do you know?"

"Because I *know*."

The door was closed. Quinton started heading back.

"But who's the you who knows?"

Hugo was looking a little less contented now. "I'm not getting it."

"Think about it. Are you the you who knows, or are you the you who knows you know?"

"You're making scant sense, Mr. McShane."

"Or are you the you who knows you know you know who you are?"

Quinton was glaring at me, evidently not appreciating this line of questioning. He reached inside his jacket.

I pulled the Glock out from under my hoodie and shot him right above his crossing arm, right in the dead center of his chest.

As he was taking his last tumble I swung the Glock around on the other three. Too late. Marvin already had a gun out and was aiming at me.

What happened next combined the most confusing and chaotic elements of rush hour at a Times Square subway station, a fire alarm in a psychiatric unit and rats running riot in a shithouse.

I ducked behind my crate as Marvin's spitfire ripped its edge to splinters. Dropping down, I crawled to the other end of the crate and went to fire. A tsunami of bullets drove me back. Three guns. They were all armed.

I ran back to the other end of the crate and fired blind into the warehouse. The second, stronger wave of the tsunami hit, gunfire coming from three different directions, shots ricocheting off the steel shipping containers and the old metal desk, everything echoing off the walls. It sounded like a gunfight in a tunnel.

More shots, then a small popping explosion, a small *ssss*. One of us had accidentally hit one of the generators. I could hear it fade out, a dying drone, like a muezzin having a heart attack in the minaret.

The overhead lights went off. The whole warehouse went into deeper darkness. The only light came from those dim mesh-covered bulbs on the walls, which practically speaking was no light at all.

This was good and bad. They couldn't see me. On the other hand, I couldn't see them.

I crouched in the shadows, trying to see figures moving in the dark, hearing running footsteps, somebody slipping on the poles on the floor, struggling to get to his or her feet, hard rounds of shattering gunfire. This was like being caught in a guerilla skirmish.

I kept moving from crate to crate. But so were they. I could hear them working their way around me, cutting me off.

"Keep your, keep your head on," Marvin yelled to me. "Put that thing down, everything, everything will be cool."

Sure it will.

I could just make out the bay door, at least get a vague sense of where it was. I began moving that way, soft stepping. The old tap dancer I'd interviewed had showed me how to do the soft shoe. Brush the ground with the balls of your feet. Swipe with the balls, not the heels, as you go forward.

At the wall I felt around for the pendant switchbox, hoping it still had power, was hooked into one of the still-running generators.

I pressed the up button and ran like hell. As the door started to lift a whole fucking fusillade of bullets pounded the space where the switchbox was hanging.

I took cover on the side of my rental. They were still firing at the switchbox, at where I'd been, when I opened the passenger door and slid inside. I stretched across the seat, keeping the door open, keeping my head below window level, groping for my keys and somehow managing to crouch underneath the steering wheel. It was as cramped as the inside of Sputnik.

Ignition. Gear shift. Gas pedal. All systems go.

The car coasted a few feet then lurched in to speed. Yelling behind me, shattering window glass, gunshot thumps shuddering into the back of the car.

Still in a fetal position, I raised my eyes just above the windshield rim and steered for the opening bay door. A thought occurred to me as I reached the night. Our happy, happy shirts were worn to shreds.

>>>

# >>>CHAPTER 6

## >>LISTEN CAREFULLY

### I THINK I SEE SOMETHING

A bunch of staffers were huddled around a monitor in the bureau's photo department. Much excitement. Last night's pap photos of the actress Kiki Ross had just come in. She'd been in rehab and hadn't gotten herself seen in a while. I was interested. There were a lot of parallels between Kiki Ross and Amanda Eston. Both had become famous in their early years, both had gone through the gauntlet of well-publicized drug and drinking problems.

Kiki *did* look good. Everyone agreed.

"She hasn't looked this good in years," one of the staffers said.

"She looks good for her age," said another.

I just up and snapped. "She looks good for her *age*?" I said. "She's *21* fucking years old!"

Okay, I was in a lousy mood.

I went back to my temporary office. Pouring rain outside, mists swirling up here at the 19th-floor level like clothes on tumble cycle.

Yes, the weather perfectly matched the state of my head.

I'd put up with all that shit last night, and had I come any closer to the truth? Not by a fucking millimeter. It had all been one totally piss-shot try.

What made me feel a little better an hour later was getting a call from Pear Wicinski. I genuinely liked her. I was glad to hear from her.

How was her back?

Getting much better. She was rubbing hot chili sauce on the afflicted area, an old remedy they'd used on the wrestling circuit.

But Pear wasn't calling to chew the fat.

*I've been looking at this awful thing again, the video. I think, I think I see something. I hadn't noticed it or hadn't seen it before, but I'm seeing it now. I think I've found something.*

"What is it?"

*I'll be honest, I'm not comfortable talking about this on the phone. It's a…it's not something I care to discuss over the lines. Do you mind coming over?*

"Not at all."

*I need another set of eyes. Maybe you can look at it, put a little gummy on it and stick it all together for me.*

"When's good?"

*Now. Now would be best. I might...right now would be best. This is something, it really shouldn't be mentioned on the phone.*

Man, *everybody's* getting paranoid.

>>>

## I KNOW WHAT YOU'VE SEEN

The rain fell so hard you could see it bouncing off the stone of Pear's Huntington Park building. I ran for the front door, hoping for a quick buzz-in and some dry shelter. Wasn't happening. I pressed, I pressed, I pressed. No answer. Strange—she'd specifically said *right now*.

Time for a mass-pressing. I mashed down on all the buttons. The door opened with a snippy click.

Everything in the hallway was the same—the bare bulbs, the old sprinkler pipes, the pee and tobacco infusion of the wood. A child was crying in one of the upper floors. I caught the sweet smell of someone doing laundry.

A9—I rang the bell, I knocked. No sounds from inside. Worried? Yes.

The lock was a decades-old make. Nobody was in the hall. I took out my laminated *Real Story* ID card—nice and flexible—slid it into the doorframe and a minute later let myself in. The tap dancer could tell you, old skills are never forgotten.

Pear was gone. Nothing had been disturbed: The crush of furniture, the belts and medals—everything was in place. But she wasn't here. How much sense did this make?

The big red bottle of Kriss-Mist still sat on the coffee table. Next to it, a glass of the all-natural laxative had already been poured. The ceiling fan had been left on. Wherever she'd gone, it was in a hurry.

A small nesting table stood under a poster giving The Wild Wicinski top billing. The phone on the table was blinking—a message she hadn't erased.

I hit *play*. The voicemail had clocked in 16 minutes ago. An old man's voice came on.

*I know what you've seen. I know all about what you've seen. I want to tell you about it. I have information you'll need. It won't take long. You'll know where to meet me. Listen carefully. You don't want to pass this by. You don't want to see anyone shop it around, and you don't want to hear it second-hand. You don't want to see it sold again. After all that's happened, you don't want to see it resold. Do you understand? I'll be waiting—it won't take long. But I can't promise I'll wait forever. So hurry.*

I played it again, only this time I made a copy on my cell. Of all the strange calls I'd heard over the last few days, this one had to rank right up there.

>>>

I studied the tape in my car, rain drenching the windshield, listening to the thing over and over. Who was the old man? Ken Hagler, the father-in-law? Fuck do I know?

I just kept replaying it, especially the *you don't want to* part. This was the strangest section of the tape. There was just something randomly rhetorical about it.

*You don't want to pass this by. You don't want to see anyone shop it around, and you don't want to hear it second-hand. You don't want to see it sold again. After all that's happened, you don't want to see it resold. Do you understand?*

What did it mean? I mean, I had a general sense of what the old man was telling her—get it now—but why was it so weirdly worded? The repeated, insistent *you don't want to* sentence structure was bothering me. Particularly since it followed him saying, *You'll know where to meet me. Listen carefully.* Could it be some kind of code? A coded message that she'd understand? Or was I trying to read too much into this?

*You don't want to see anyone shop it around, and you don't want to hear it second-hand. You don't want to see it sold again. After all that's happened, you don't want to see it resold.*

I remembered something. Pear and I were walking along the streets, passing stores that sold liquor, take-out, herbs, religion, and at one point we went past a second-hand clothing called The ReSouled Shop.

*You don't want to see anyone SHOP it around.*

*You don't want to hear it SECOND-HAND.*

*You don't want to see it RESOLD.*

It was on her usual route. Every day she'd *pass it by.*

*Do you understand?* Fucking A.

It's true, there really *is* no cure for the common code.


>>>

## RESOULED

Traffic in the downpour was a slow-go both ways. Three blocks from The ReSouled Shop I finally decided to fuck-it park and get out. I couldn't see or hear anything, but something already felt off.

I ran through the wet haze, the winds carrying the stink of gasoline off the Harbor Freeway. A crowd had formed on the side of the shop.

The next store over sold Mexican handicrafts and cell phones. A tiny yard separated the two buildings. I wedged through the bystanders.

The yard was a dirt-packed square of land with a grand total of one tree. The surrounding walls were covered with peeling paint and the spiders of overgrown vines. If forgotten angels needed a place to congregate, they'd hang here.

Blood had splattered against one of the walls and left a trail to the body on the ground. I could see the broad shoulders under a pink floral raincoat. I could see blood and a bullet gouge on her broad face. Pear's cane had fallen a few feet away.

My heart fell to the bottom of my stomach.

A man stood next to me wearing a ReSouled T-shirt. I asked what happened.

"No idea. I was next door, heard shots. Ran out, found her."

Radio static popped behind us. A policewoman in a slicker told us to clear out. "We need to rope this off. Everybody get back."

I stood with the crowd. The whole city was a stunned wet white. There was a furious need, a desperate electricity in the soaked air.

Enough. Enough, enough, enough. I was tired of waiting for the truth to come to me. I had to go after it. I had to go to the source. I knew that now with the conviction of a clenched fist.

Gold help me—and I mean that literally—I was going to do it.

**CORRIDOR VII**

It was getting dark by the time I landed in Reno. I rented a car, took Interstate 80 and parked a quarter-mile away from the white granite mountain with the house mutating at its base. I changed my clothes in the night. Black pants, black T, black soft-soled shoes, black utility belt. The belt I stocked with the goodies bought on the shopping spree I'd made before leaving LA.

Time to crash over the edge.

I walked slowly along the high, gapless granite wall that guarded the front of the house, doing a midnight creep—or a 10 p.m. creep—until I reached the far end. The area by the entrance to the tunnel was lit now by a field of floodlights. Only one way to get it done—I ran for it, weaving through the shadows cast by the floods until I got to the mountain wall.

I slid along the stone, getting closer
to the entrance, eyes searching every inch
for hidden motion detectors. Nothing. So
far this was as smooth as a new razor.

The barrier at the entrance was
down. No cars approaching, no guards
around. I ducked under the barrier and,
staying double-bent, slipped up against the
inside wall.

Here it all was again—the maze of
passageways carved into the bottom of the
mountain, the eerie light of the high bays,
the khaki-uniformed guards with their
holsters at their sides. I counted six on
duty, two watching the flashing lights of
display panels, the others laughing and
fucking around. All of their lapel-attached
walkie-talkies were silent. A quiet night in
the cave.

I moved along the wall—balls of
my feet, the old soft shoe—edging toward

the tunnel I'd taken my first time here. I saw now that the passageway had an official designation: Corridor VII. Roman numerals—so pretentious.

A hundred and fifty feet of baptismal white granite stretched in front of me. The tunnel's lights were low, dim gray. I continued my wall-creeping, breathing steady, concentration full but relaxed. A calmly alert attitude in a situation like this was as important as the Glock in the back band of my pants.

I passed a few utility doors until I found the one I wanted: Electrical. The lock was one of the Hadcock 2000 series. I took a pick set out of my belt, slipped the prongs inside the keyhole and let my fingers do the talking. Forty seconds later the door opened.

Inside. Close the door. Fumble in the dark for the miniature flashlight on my belt. Its light showed dozens of circuit boxes, all neatly labeled. I settled for the one that said Alarms. Big box, lotta wiring. But every circuit was identified. Very efficient, very accommodating.

I found V, VI, VII, pulled a pair of jeweler's cutting pliers off my belt. Corridor VII was connected by three wires, a patriotic red, white and blue.

I snipped the red, waited to hear a tampering alarm. Nothing went off. I cut the white and the blue. Nothing. No guards scrambling down the tunnel with their guns drawn.

I stepped out and quietly shut the door. The corridor was silent.

It stayed that way as I kept moving. Just ahead was the brass-grilled door that lead into the house. I slowly grabbed the knob and pulled it open. No alarms, completely disabled. The only thing I could hear was my heart pounding in my head.

I was inside the wide hallway, a library-study and a couple of guest bedrooms lining the wall that didn't touch the mountain. All their doors were closed.

A sound was coming from the library-study. Maybe a voice. I moved closer, went to reach for the knob. No, not a voice. *Voices*, muffled voices from inside. At least three people. I took out the Glock, took a deep breath and put my hand around the knob.

Then I heard something I didn't expect. Music. A swell of dramatic, portentous music, a signal of danger, building in the lower registers and then suddenly rising to an ominous crescendo.

>>>

## NOTHING PERSONAL

He was watching a movie. *Pirates of the Caribbean*. The first one, *The Curse of the Black Pearl*. Or actually he *wasn't* watching it. Robby was sitting at his desktop, casual in shorts and a purple silk T, trying to type something out on the keyboard while Johnny Depp, Orlando Bloom and Kiera Knightly went through some kind of tense confrontation on the screen behind him.

Robby turned, looked at me, the Glock, and slowly shook his head. "You're a confident son of a bitch, aren't you?"

"When circumstances dictate."

Back to hunting and pecking. "I've already talked to you."

"We're not finished. Far from it."

Nice room. Leather furniture, recessed lighting, its own bathroom. A piece of sculpture, a slab of white granite carved in a graceful face-down half moon, was hanging on the wall. In the yard just outside was a rock formation with the same curve as the sculpture, giving the impression that both were made by the same hand.

"You seem pretty angry," he said.

"I *am* pretty angry."

"Well you don't have to be *that* angry."

"You're telling me how angry I should be? I'm *angry*."

"Take my word for it, you're coming off *very* angry. Even kinda crazy."

He was sitting in a rolling armchair. I yanked the chair and all 6-4 of him away from the desk. I pulled him into the middle of the room, away from anything he could touch to alert the guards.

I raised the Glock to his eyes. "This'll put you out forever."

He ran his fingers through his Kennedy hair. "What's with you? You think you're better than me?"

"Probably worse, but it's not about me. It's been you all along, hasn't it? It's always been you."

"I need the video. I really, really need it."

"It's been you, right? The warehouse, the parking garage, Santa Monica?"

Robby lifted his shoulders and sighed for all of America. "I hired people. I hired people to get it. I have the resources, I have the connections." He turned both hands palms up—that's the way it works.

"Since Amsterdam? Since Arnoud Shuyler?"

"Sorry for the trouble. It was nothing personal."

Listen to him. "Why do you need the video?"

"This is really depressing."

"Why do you need it!"

"Because I *need* it! Because my fucking *life* depends on it!"

I pressed the Glock right against his forehead. I could feel the sensation of the steel sprawl across his face, run down his neck and spread to his heart.

"*Why?*"

He searched his mind for something to say. All he could find were yellow sagebrush flowers and beaded Paiute baskets.

"It's me," he said. "It's me in the video. With Amanda."

I took the gun away from his head. "You were gonna have your lawyer lie?

You were gonna have your wife swear it wasn't your birthmark?"

"It wasn't a lie. It was just a little less than the truth."

"How so?"

"I had it removed. I had the birthmark removed. When I was in prison. Nothing else to do in there. It's just something, you know, I was always a little sensitive about."

God, stop me from murdering this man.

"So you want the video."

"I *need* the video."

"So nobody will know you killed her?"

"I didn't. I did *not* do that. I was there, yes I was, but don't, you know, on the basis of that, don't jump to any of these audacious, grandiose L.C. Martin conclusions."

"Why the fuck not?"

"Cause Amanda, I liked her, I absolutely liked her, but it was just a *thing*. That's all it was."

"A thing."

"That's it—nothing serious. Her life, you know, her life was an upside-down turmoil. Just *thinking* about it is nerve-wracking."

"That's a real tragedy."

"I don't know what it is, but it was fucked-up. Much as I liked her, I couldn't get *deep* into a situation like that. It was just a thing."

"You have no fucking feelings."

"You're wrong. I've got *too* many feelings, that's my problem."

"Meaning?"

Robby sat in the chair, wondering what he was supposed to be feeling at this moment.

"I have an alibi," he said in a voice as quiet as I'd ever heard out of him. "I have an alibi for later that night. For the time she died."

"What is it?"

"I guess… I guess this is the ironic part of it. Considering."

"I'm running way out of patience."

"I was with someone else that night. I was with my *other* girlfriend when Amanda died."

"Jesus, you're unbelievable. Who was she?"

"Her name's Lisa Kohler. She lives here. In town."

"She'll vouch for you?"

Robby nodded. "We were together that night. We were together when the news came out. I remember."

"Will *she* remember?"

"She remembers."

"And you know this how?"

"We're still together. We've been together all this time. We have two kids together."

"You really get around, don't you?"

"That's why I want the video. I'm trying to protect her. Her and myself."

"From?"

"Who do you think? From Ken. From my father-in-law. He finds out about Lisa and the kids, he'll kick me out faster than light. Or he'll do worse, at least. If he and my wife find out about Lisa, I'll lose everything. That's why I need the video. So I don't *have* to produce an alibi. So I don't have to tell *anyone* about Lisa."

He had tears in his eyes. Probably very rare for someone like Robby Walsh to cry.

Proof, once more, that God believes in ironic retribution.

I almost believed him.

"So you were with this Lisa Kohler that night."

"I was. You can ask."

"But you could've hired the job out."

"No. I could never hurt Amanda. I could never hurt someone I felt that way about. I don't think I could ever do that."

"Don't get so morose. You've got a track record for hiring scum."

"To *scare* people, yeah. To scare *you* into giving the video up. But someone like Amanda, no."

"How about someone like Pear Wicinski? Why her?"

His eyes took a strange twist. "*Who*? You mean the old bodyguard? The old wrestler?'

"The same."

"That was meant for *you* the other day. Squeeze some *pressure* on you. I didn't mean for her to be part of it."

"I mean this morning. You had her killed this morning."

"I *what*?" He nearly jumped out of the chair. "What? When? Where?"

"Huntington Park. You had her shot."

"*No*. I would never do that." His eyes were red with tears, strain and confusion. "I *liked* her, I liked Pear. I remember her from those days. I liked all her old stories. I would never kill someone I liked."

Amazing turn of logic there. And I believed it.

I believed him.

>>>

# >>>CHAPTER 7

## >>DEATH WATCH

### JUST BEFORE THE WORLD ENDS

I spent the night in Reno, setting out the next morning to find Lisa Kohler and confirm Robby's alibi. She lived in a condo development near the Firecreek Crossing Mall, and it was not a romantic vision. Lisa was a bitter, heavyset woman with a bubble butt and mascara so thick it seemed to be squeezing the eyeballs out of her head. Yes, Robby had told her I might be coming around, he'd called. Of course, he couldn't come *here* and tell her to her face. No, that didn't go with the goddamn territory, and frankly she was sick of it. She was tired of the way things were after five fucking years, seeing him only here and there, waiting for him while he did his federal time and still he spends most of the time with that bitch-wife Leah Hagler Walsh? Is this a way to live?

I caught a glimpse of two young children in the kitchen, trying to cobble peanut butter and jelly sandwiches together for breakfast.

But she *did* back Robby's story.

"The fact of the matter is, I was with him all that night. No confabulation. I'll swear to it in court if I have to."

"And when the news broke, Amanda Eston was dead, you were still with him?"

Lisa produced something between a laugh and a snort. "She was lucky."

"Lucky?"

"Some people think life is this wonderful thing. I don't, not really. Tell you the truth, life isn't particularly to my liking."

Have to say, Lisa was not my type, but to each his or her own.

I can just *imagine* what Robby's wife was like.

>>>

I kept watching the video. On the flight back, all that day, I kept going over the same minute and 18 seconds of tape. I kept thinking about what Pear said when she'd called. *I've been looking at this awful thing again, the video. I think I see something. I hadn't noticed it or hadn't seen it before, but I'm seeing it now. I think I've found something.*

I kept replaying the voicemail I'd found on her phone, the old man telling her, *I know what you've seen. I know all about what you've seen.*

And what the hell was *that*?

All I could see were the same dim blurs, the same grainy shadows. All I could see was Amanda, her mermaid tattoo, her Blistexed lips, her brown mole just above the left side of her mouth. All I could see was the torso of the man I knew now was Robby Walsh, his wine-colored birthmark disappearing in her mouth. All I could see were the smudged patches of darkness that felt like a prophecy of the moment of death.

You stare at 1:18 minutes of video long enough, you get dizzy and disoriented. But I couldn't stop looking.

Something was hidden on the screen, some message was transmitting from that night. Another code, but one I couldn't decipher. A message so spectral and smoky it didn't even leave a shadow.

There'd been a veiled sun in the sky all that day, a sultry, yellowish-gray light that never changed. This is probably the way things will look just before the world ends.

Pear's words: *I hadn't noticed it or hadn't seen if before, but I'm seeing it now.* Why hadn't she noticed it before? Because it wasn't obvious. And why wasn't it obvious?

Because both of us had been looking in the foreground and not the background? Lots of things can get lost because we only target the figure and not the setting. Because our eyes tend to pass over the background.

But what was in the background here? Just the TV, rippling with videoed static lines, and an out-of-focus bunch of jewelry left on the counter next to it. How many secrets could be found in the TV? Probably not many, not in a KTTV newscast that had been seen by thousands of people the night it aired. But the jewelry?

I made a frame grab off the tape and began zooming it up. At 20% I could start to make out the outlines of necklaces and bracelets, clumps of what might've been earrings and rings. At 30% I could see something else in the middle of the pile. Something larger than the rest, something with an octagonal shape.

That meant something. Something about an octagon was tagged in my brain.

I remembered eating lunch at Reggie's on Robertson, remembered L.C. Martin's Gucci suit, his diamond-studded cufflinks, and just beneath the sleeve of his Hilditch & Key shirt, an octagonally shaped watch.

I brought the image up to 40%, the point where the resolution was just about to break up and completely go. But I could see it—L.C.'s rare, expensive, impossible-to-get Fleischer-Koch octagonally faced watch.

I remembered something else from that lunch. I remembered L.C. telling me he hadn't seen Amanda for three or four days before she died.

So what was his rare, expensive, impossible-to-get Fleischer-Koch watch doing in her bedroom that night?

>>>

And as I kept asking myself that question, another idea came to me. I played the voicemail again, the old man telling Pear, *I know what you've seen. I know all about what you've seen.*

It was a long day, night was setting in. I was wired and picking up all kinds of bizarre frequencies. But I still couldn't stop.

I went to a movie rental site and downloaded a copy of *Days of Reckoning*. This was the film where Amanda tries to return to her father after a long separation, and in the course of getting back together she imagines the man in all stages of his former life.

Her father was played by an actor her own age, a slightly talented, all-but-forgotten name from a reality series, L.C. Martin. Most people regarded his casting as a demented joke, but he gave a tremendous performance, aging from a wiseass teen to a withered senior with a grasp and understanding that won him an Oscar nomination as Best Supporting Actor.

This is where he'd met Amanda, making *Days of Reckoning*. They were married the day the movie wrapped, right on the set, in the place where he'd delivered the best film work he'd ever done, the best he'd ever do.

I fast-forwarded the movie, jumping to the scene where Amanda first shows up at her old house. L.C. comes to the door, recognizes her after a moment and isn't happy about it. She starts to tell him why she's suddenly showing up after all this time. He holds up a hand, stops her.

L.C.: *Don't bother explaining. I know.*

Amanda: *How can you know?*

L.C.: *You still think I'm stupid? I know why you're here. I know all about why you're here.*

I went back to the voicemail. Same pitch, same timbre, same breathing patterns, same trembling crack in the old man's voice.

It was his best performance.


>>>

## NIGHT OF RECKONING

At *Real Story* we track traffic on our site with a heat map, a piece of graphic software that lets you see in real time what photos, videos, headlines and stories are getting the most hits. The hot spot on my own personal heat map was 58 Chenille Lane, Beverly Glen. L.C.'s home. My friend Kumiko Davis had given me the address what seemed like a long time ago.

The house was a Mid Century Modern, one of those Frank Lloyd Wright-like structures located down a long slope of land, its low sling roof supported by big slabs of wood and stone and big rectangles of glass. Welcome to the Atomic Age. There were no lights on inside, but a Mercedes SL was parked in the driveway.

I moved through the border of pines in the front and slid along the walls. Just like last night I was dressed all in black, complete with the utility belt. Big slice of moon in the clear sky, plus Venus, the evening/morning star.

All the factors were converging.

The lock: a Camtone Biaxial. Picking wasn't easy. It took me six minutes and many tries. I opened the door, stepped inside, shut it and immediately looked for the keypad, needing to disarm it before the alarm went off.

Thing was, security hadn't been activated. The system was already off. No one had set the alarm, either out of perverse negligence...

...or because the bills hadn't been paid.

I was tending toward the latter explanation when I turned the miniature flashlight on the interior of the house. I saw a huge open-floor living room, bulky sectionals, aluminum pole lamps, ceramic vases. But everything was going to filthy ruin. Dirty dishes, half-eaten sandwiches, teetering piles of junk, garbage left everywhere, the furniture once good and now threadbare, the walnut floors scratched and scuffed, coffee cups crusted with dirt, half full glasses (or, in this case, half empty). And an odor that almost smelled like—yeah, there it was, the pungent kick of urine.

L.C. had told me he was a successful producer of corporate videos. So why was he living like a crazed animal?

Some house. All put-together outside, all squatter chaos inside.

I remembered the reviews of his reality series, *The Pre-Life*, where the cast was supposed to be struggling first-year pre-med students. How much of this reality, the critics asked, was really real?

I took a few steps into the living room. My foot hit something—a spent soup can. It rolled into the wall and echoed through the big empty space.

Breathe, concentrate.

I ran the flashlight over the walls. Textured surfaces, Venetian plaster. Glass-framed photos on one wall. All of Amanda. Either her alone or with him. Just below the photos, the wall was smeared with some kind of fudgy residue.

"What the hell *is* this?"

I spun the light around to the voice. L.C., all the way over on the opposite side of the room, standing in the other entrance. He was still wearing the Fleischer-Koch watch on his left wrist. He was holding a small, blue-finish gun in his right hand, a Bersa Thunder 9 mm.

It was his eyes, though, that really got my attention. They were as black rimmed as a raccoon's, like he hadn't slept in months. But his irises were sharp and alert, as sharp as starlight.

"Is that you?" he said.

"Is that who?"

"*You*. McShane."

"It's me. What's the matter with you? You look terrible."

No answer, just a shake of the head.

"Are you sick?"

He closed his eyes for a long moment. "I haven't felt well in five years."

He took exactly one step into the living room. No Gucci now. He was wearing a pair of jeans and a denim shirt with orange-yellow stains—possibly cheese—all down the front.

This was the real L.C. Martin. The person I'd met for lunch, that was a performance.

"Nice place," I said.

"You think?"

"Little run-down, though, no?"

"It'll do. I don't need a lot of fancy-schmancy."

"Well you need *something*."

He suddenly blew up. "*Nobody* can tell me what I need! *Nobody*! You want to start giving me advice, don't bother. Every word's going down the bowl and getting flushed away."

He closed his eyes again, shook his head, then took a look around the place. It was like he was orienting himself, starting over, trying to figure out where he was. Or who he was.

"Turn that off." He pointed the Bersa at the flashlight.

"Why?"

"It's right in my fucking face. You've seen enough."

"I feel safer this way."

"It's *bothering* me."

I shut the light and immediately put my hand on my Glock. But he didn't try anything. He didn't fire. We just stood there on opposite sides of the room, letting our eyes adjust to the moonlit darkness.

"Nice watch you have there," I said.

No response. Then: "Amanda gave it to me. It was a gift."

"When'd she give it to you?"

"When we started going out."

"*Days of Reckoning*, right? Back then?"

"Right."

"Do the voice again."

"What voice?"

"Your voice, from *Days of Reckoning*."

"Why should I? Why bother?"

"Cause it sounded pretty good on Pear's voicemail. Sounded like you haven't missed a beat."

I could just make him out in the low light, but I could see him getting twitchy and fidgety. It was just like the lunch, when he'd looked like he was going into a nicotine fit.

"I have to tell you," he said, "I might've had something to do with that."

"I *know* you did. Question is why?"

"Pear kind of a, she hit—what do they call it? She hit a raw nerve."

"What raw nerve?"

"She called me, said she'd seen something in the video. Said get your ass over here right now. She said you were going to be there too. The way she said it, sounded like she was going to bust me in front of you."

"That watch was gonna get you in trouble."

"It made things messy. So I called back couple minutes later. She didn't pick up, in the bathroom or something. I left a message."

"Doing the voice."

L.C. shrugged. "I wanted to sound like someone who had a secret to tell. I wanted to add an air of mystery, sound like someone who didn't want to be exposed."

"So the coded message. The ReSouled Shop."

"I'd walked with her to the store many times. I knew the way. I knew she'd know."

"And you killed her."

"Her problem? She never listened. She *never* listened to me. I'd talk and talk? Was all nah-nah-nah to her. Well it's too

late for nah-nah-nah. It's too late for all
that not-listening shit."

"Why too late?"

"Cause it has to happen *now*.
We've all been waiting too long—right
*now*. Somebody around here needs to tell
the truth. Somebody needs to start telling
the truth and it needs to start right fucking
*now*!"

I saw him raise the Bersa in this
direction. Better not wait to see what
would happen.

I dove in back of the nearest
sectional, heard three ear-paralyzing
explosions and I swear I could feel the
force of the bullets as they flashed over
my head and smashed into something
behind me. Glass shattered and crashed to
the floor. Amanda's photos.

I took the Glock out.

"You weren't listening to me!" he yelled.

His voice was coming from a different place now, closer to the ground. He'd ducked behind the sectional directly across the room from mine.

"When we met," L.C. said, "the whole time we talked, you were never listening to me!"

"I was."

"*Weren't!*"

Two more Bersa shots from him. You could hear them echo through the house.

Heat waves were rising up the back of my skull, where sweat forms in stress-time.

Another sectional was in front of me, at a right angle to mine. If I could make it over there, I'd be closer to him, get a better shot.

I fired, jumped out, ran while I kept firing and belly-flopped behind the other sectional. L.C. threw three more loud-to-terrifying shots. Ceramic vases shattered and fell all around me.

My strategy, as they say, was evolving.

"You don't understand how *big* this is," he said, "how *wide*. I told you before, you can't see the *dimensions* of this thing."

"You sure?"

"You have no idea. You have no fucking idea how far the *scope* of this thing goes."

"You ever listen to yourself?"

"All the time."

"Listen *harder*."

L.C. replied with two shots that thudded into the sectional and knocked it back by a foot.

I needed to get even closer, get a better angle on him. Another sectional sat six feet away, with an aluminum pole lamp by its side. I slipped out from my cover and set off another shitstorm of gunfire while I ran

He won't get fooled again.

L.C. fired three times. Two of the bullets slammed into the wall behind me. I didn't hear the third—it went into my thigh with a dull silence.

For a moment I was more surprised than anything else. I just stood there. Then the pain set in. It felt like a 10-inch nail had been driven into my leg. I lost everything. All my weight fell to my feet. The Glock dropped out of my hand. I stumbled into the pole lamp, toppled over with it and went down flat on my back.

I heard L.C. moving. The Glock was three feet away, on the other side of the lamp. I stretched for the gun but I couldn't reach it. Too much pain, too much stun. I couldn't get my hand past the lamp.

L.C. was standing in front of me.

"You're scaring me," he said. "It scares me to think that the whole time we talked that time, you were never paying attention to anything I said."

"I paid attention."

"If you *had* paid attention, you wouldn't *be* here right now."

He aimed the Bersa. I couldn't get much leverage on my back, but I swung the lamp with everything I had. The pole caught him on the side of his head and spun him around. Two shots hit the floor as he staggered to stay on his feet.

I pushed through the pain and grabbed the Glock, swung around as he came back. Only one shot open from this dust-level angle. I couldn't get it up, so I put the bullet in his kneecap.

His scream sounded like a car trying to brake at 140 mph.

>>>

Our blood was all over the floor. We were both sitting in it, propped up with our backs against the sectionals. I had the Glock on him. His face was pinched with pain, eyes wasting away. He looked like a brain scan come to life.

He was gasping for breath, but it didn't stop him from carrying on. "I can't believe people. It's like they're lost in this haze, this mental smog. And you try to pull them out, and I've tried, I've pushed my efforts to the fucking edge, they still keep walking around blind. And you know what? You know something? I think I'm gonna pass out."

"Stay with me."

"Stay with you. Look at this knee. It *hurts!* You wouldn't believe how much it *hurts!*"

"I'd believe it. Look at my leg."

"Your leg? Fuck your leg. It's my fucking *knee!*"

He kinda had a point. My thigh wound wasn't as bad. I could barely move it, but at least the pain wasn't so knifey anymore. Adrenaline is a great painkiller.

L.C. picked something off the floor. An empty cereal box, one of those mini Cheerios boxes from a Valu-Pak. He stared at it like he'd never seen one before.

"I don't know if things necessarily pertain to me anymore."

I pointed the Glock at him. "This pertains to you. Talk to me."

"About what?"

"About Amanda, what do you think?"

"There's no profit in that." He put the box down and carefully touched the area around his knee. Then he wiped his hand on his shirt, smearing more blood into the leftover cheese stains. "There's no profit in that whatsoever."

"I want to know who killed her."

"You *know* who killed her."

"That's right. I *do*. I want to know *why*."

"Then fucking *ask* him. Fucking ask that out of control jerk off."

"Robby?"

"Who the fuck else?"

"Boo. Hiss."

"Problem?"

"There's no blood left in that stone. Pardon the expression."

"Well there's plenty of shit left. And whatever shit that offensive piece of vermin was involved in, that's a private matter between him and his asshole."

"You know he's a real human being, right? He actually exists? He's not some fantasy in your head? Some abstraction?"

"Whatever he is, it's his fault."

"How?"

L.C. lapsed into more of those twitchy fidgets, but weaker now, sicklier, like a junkie who'd only tasted a small dose of what he needed.

"You saw the video," he said. "He was *there* that night. That's why it's his fault. He was *there* with her."

"So they were seeing each other. Public knowledge."

"So I was *staying* there at the time. I was *living* there. Had to go out for a few hours, and the minute I'm gone he's in there fucking his head off."

"That's what your watch was doing there, in the bedroom."

"With my *watch* in there they're doing it! With my fucking *watch* in the same room they're, they're making *smoochies* or whatever, I don't know."

"How'd you know he was there?"

"Cause I'm a fucking mind-reader. She *told* me. She admitted it when I got back. She said he'd just been there. She'd just been with him." He shook his head like the thing was beyond comprehension. "She said she'd decided we shouldn't be getting back together. She'd made up her mind. She said she didn't want to get married again."

I could hear his heart pounding from over here.

"Then what happened?"

"*Then* what? You know what it's like when something you think shouldn't be real turns out to be the *only* thing that's real?"

"Actually I do."

"Then listen to me. If you listen to only one thing I have to say, listen to this. I needed her. I was crushed down by how much I needed her. I was worth nothing without her. I was, I mean *look* at me—I *am* worth nothing without her. Even as an actor, shit, even as an actor, I was only good with her."

"*Days of Reckoning.*"

He nodded, glanced at his knee. "This thing is killing me. I think I'm gonna faint."

"Finish talking. What happened that night?"

"That night. I went out again that night. She went to bed. I drove around. I got pissed. I got so pissed. I had these things in my head they were splitting my brain apart. I had these things in my head I didn't know what to do about them. I didn't know. I just didn't know. All my prayers were gone, I didn't know what to do."

"When did you decide to kill her?"

"Not sure I ever did. Not sure I ever worked it out to where I could use those words, where I could say those words to myself."

I believed it. His voice was becoming soft and almost incredulous, like he couldn't believe the things that were coming out of his own mouth.

"I drove to a guy I used to know, from the old days, from my club days. He used to sell pralicin as a cheap fuck-drug."

"You knew what it could do?"

"My father was a pharmacist. I knew. My father, that's how I got cast in *The Pre-Life*. Remember that show?"

"I remember."

"I got home, she was asleep. Just laying there. I shot her up. I'd bought a tiny butterfly syringe from the guy too. You skin-pop it, it hardly leaves a mark. I shot her up, I packed my stuff, I left. She'd turned me into nothing. I did the same for her."

I could've killed him. I could've easily shot him right there, just like I'd shot that junkie bastard years ago. Wouldn't even have to move the Glock. Just pull the trigger.

But I couldn't do it. Looking at him propped up there, looking at the reality of his life, the dirt, the garbage, the haunted mess, I couldn't do it. He was just too pathetic.

"I'm not mad at her anymore," he said. "Was for a while, but not anymore. You look at it in retrospect, what happened that night, it was almost like— what's the word? There's a word for when things like this happen. You know what it is. It's a word—it's not coming to me."

"I don't know what it is."

"It's a *common* word. People use it all the time. It's almost like fate. It's— wait, it *is* fate. That's what it is, it's *fate*. It's fate except, except when you think about it, what *is* fate? You know? When you actually *look* at it, what the fuck *is* fate?"

Talking to him was like trying to wrap madness in a rubber band.

He touched his leg again, wiped blood on his shirt. "I have to tell you something. I'm feeling really bad. This thing's really hurting. I'm starting to fade out."

"Go ahead. Close your eyes. Let yourself go."

He pulled the cheese and blood stained shirt up to his chin. It was like he was trying to crawl inside his clothes.

"I don't know what happened to her," he said. "I've tried to understand, I owe her that much, but I can't. We were so happy. *She* was so happy. But she couldn't seem to stay that way. Like she was *allergic* to it. Something just ate away at her, something devoured her, and everything just turned to shit."

He closed his eyes.

"Give into it," I said. "Take a rest. Just let it go."

>>>

It was a strange thing to see. Eventually L.C. passed out, but he still had tears falling down his face. A flood of large, painful tears. He was unconscious, but he was involuntarily crying. The flood was almost Shakespearean—Lear's tears, they scald like molten lead.

I checked my cell. Everything he'd told me was on tape.

I rewound, went back. Everything Robby Walsh had told me was on tape.

That's when I finally called the police.

>>>

## LIKE SOMEONE CRYING

Amanda Eston was buried in a pink marble garden crypt, surrounded by a lawn that was probably as trimmed and green as a U.S. Open course. You couldn't tell today, though, because the grass was filled with flowers and stuffed animals and candles and handmade cards. With censored parts of her full video getting millions of hits a day on the *Real Story* site, she'd been officially rediscovered. Signs of her renewed celebrity, in fact, could be found all over the country: The Crazy Face label was reporting that its limited-edition Amanda Eston T-shirt had sold out.

Beautiful sunny day. Clear sky, long-leafed willow trees lining the cemetery. Tasha, smelling like mango and lavender, was carrying two wreathes made of marigolds. I was walking with a cane. I thought of it as a tribute to Pear Wicinski.

Tasha placed one of her wreathes on the grave pile. We stood staring at the marble block, the name etched on its surface.

"I keep thinking of the morning after," she said. "The morning after she died, the morning after I heard. I woke up thinking, this is the first morning of my life where my sister is no longer part of this world."

She was still shaken by L.C.'s arrest. For five years she'd believed that Amanda had taken her own life. Now she knew it wasn't true. In a twisted and tragic way, her sister had escaped the family history, eluded the genetic trap. Now Tasha had a five-year block of belief to demolish.

L.C. Martin was in jail, the medical wing, held as a suspect in the deaths of Amanda Eston and Pear Wicinski.

Robby Walsh was being investigated on various charges of conspiracy to commit assault and battery, and, with the cooperation of the van de Politie Amsterdam-Amstelland, for conspiracy in the death of Arnoud Shuyler. His wife had left him, he'd lost his lobbying jobs and he was now living in the condo near the Firecreek Crossing Mall with Lisa Kohler and their two kids.

I guess at least one person—Lisa— was happy.

Maybe Grady Alexander too. We'd made the deal for the video--$12 million. No negotiation. He'd just wanted to get it over.

"It's weird," said Tasha, "how you can caught on a thought. I thought one thing, and I got used to it. I got used to the physical sensation of it, to all the emotions attached to it."

"That's what happens. Even with an idea. You get used to it, habituated to it, addicted to it."

"So what do I do now? Is the truth better than what I thought? Is the truth better or worse? I can't decide."

"No better, no worse. It's just the truth."

"It feels pretty strange to me. It's almost something I want to hide away, cause I don't understand it."

"That strangeness? That weirdness? That's us."

We walked over to Aunt Renee's crypt nearby. Or she walked. I limped along.

I was thinking about the past and its powers to haunt. I'd once done a story

on a guy who'd shot and killed another
guy over an argument they'd had 25 years
ago. They hadn't seen each other since. So
the big question, of course, was *why* after
all this time. The guy said he'd recently
retired and had plenty of time to brood.

*But after 25 years?* I'd said.

The guy shrugged. *It always
bothered me.*

Tasha put her other wreathe at the
foot of Aunt Renee's pink marble. There
was a bench a few feet away, under the
drooping leaves of a willow tree. We sat,
Tasha looking at her sister's grave.

"Something she said to me once.
She was in one of her morbid periods, she
made me promise that if she died, I'd put
her in an open casket at the funeral. She
wanted people to see her. She always
wanted to be seen. So that's what we did.

Open casket, champagne colored lining, satin and silk."

I held her hand.

"The day was just like this," she said. "It was a beautiful ceremony. Only thing that went wrong, L.C.'d hired this woman to sing. She sounded fine for a minute or so, then her microphone went. Just completely shut down. We couldn't hear the words, but you could still her voice. Just her voice, just this sad sound. It was beautiful, maybe even more beautiful than with the words. It sounded like someone crying."

I thought about something I'd told her that first night in her apartment, about the old rites of initiation. How they all ended the same way, with an acceptance of ordinary reality, with an embrace of the everyday world.

It must've felt just like this. The willow tree was still a willow tree, but it was a tree multiplied by a million. The sun was the sun but it was more than before. The sky was the sky but it was more than before. Everything was ordinary, but unlike anything it had ever been before.

###

## WHO THE HELL WROTE THIS?

I worked as an Executive Editor at *Entertainment Weekly* for 11 years and (in two separate stints) at *People* magazine and people.com for 12 years. I often speak to young journalists and try to use myself as an example for inspiration—a guy who spent time in jail, rehab and a psych ward and somehow went on to become a successful editor at Time Inc. and managed to keep himself sane and alive. I've tried to reflect those experiences in this book.

My wife, Laurie, and I live in Garden City, N.Y.

You can visit my page @ smashwords.com/profile/view/ richardsanders

6R0

Made in the USA
Lexington, KY
10 August 2011